BELLAROO CREEK!

Three brave women, three strong men…
and one town on the brink

Bellaroo Creek in the Australian Outback
is a town in need of rescue! So the arrival of
three single women and a few adorable kids
is exactly the injection of life it needs. Are
the town and its ruggedly gorgeous cattlemen
prepared for the adventure ahead?

One town, three heart-warming romances
to cherish forever!

THE CATTLEMAN'S READY-MADE FAMILY
by Michelle Douglas
in July 2013

MIRACLE IN BELLAROO CREEK
by Barbara Hannay
in August 2013

PATCHWORK FAMILY IN THE OUTBACK
by Soraya Lane
in September 2013

Dear Reader,

You might be surprised to hear that Australia is one of the most urbanised countries in the world. Ninety percent of our population live in cities scattered around the nation's coastlines, and yet, historically, we owe our existence and success to the rural areas inland, where wheat, sheep and cattle have been farmed since early settlement—and where huge mineral deposits are also mined.

I guess it's no surprise that city dwellers love visiting our country towns with their tree-lined streets and close-knit communities and slower-paced living. I'm sure many visitors dream of going back to a less stressful, less complicated way of life, just as Milla (and subsequently Ed) have done in this story.

In Australia, we worry when we hear that these towns, that were once our country's heartbeat, are dying from decreasing populations. *Save the Town* initiatives are popping up all over Australia and we wish them the same success that Bellaroo Creek achieved.

I'm hugely grateful to Michelle Douglas and Soraya Lane for the wonderful brainstorming email chats we had while coming up with this trilogy. Their continued inspiration during the writing process was invaluable.

I hope you enjoy visiting Bellaroo Creek.

Warmest wishes,

Barbara

MIRACLE IN BELLAROO CREEK

BY
BARBARA HANNAY

First published in Great Britain 2013
by Mills & Boon, an imprint of Harlequin (UK) Limited.
Harlequin (UK) Limited, Eton House, 18-24 Paradise Road,
Richmond, Surrey TW9 1SR

© Barbara Hannay 2013

ISBN: 978 0 263 23529 6

Harlequin (UK) policy is to use papers that are natural, renewable and recyclable products and made from wood grown in sustainable forests. The logging and manufacturing process conform to the legal environmental regulations of the country of origin.

Printed and bound in Great Britain
by CPI Antony Rowe, Chippenham, Wiltshire

Reading and writing have always been a big part of **Barbara Hannay**'s life. She wrote her first short story at the age of eight for the Brownies' writer's badge. It was about a girl who was devastated when her family had to move from the city to the Australian Outback.

Since then, a love of both city and country lifestyles has been a continuing theme in Barbara's books and in her life. Although she has mostly lived in cities, now that her family has grown up and she's a full-time writer she's enjoying a country lifestyle.

Barbara and her husband live on a misty hillside in Far North Queensland's Atherton Tableland. When she's not lost in the world of her stories she's enjoying farmers' markets, gardening clubs and writing groups, or preparing for visits from family and friends.

Barbara records her country life in her blog, *Barbwired*, and her website is: www.barbarahannay.com

Recent books by Barbara Hannay:

THE CATTLEMAN'S SPECIAL DELIVERY
FALLING FOR MR MYSTERIOUS
RUNAWAY BRIDE
BRIDESMAID SAYS, 'I DO!'
RANCHER'S TWINS: MUM NEEEDED
MOLLY COOPER'S DREAM DATE
A MIRACLE FOR HIS SECRET SON
EXECUTIVE: EXPECTING TINY TWINS
THE CATTLEMAN'S ADOPTED FAMILY

Did you know these are also available as eBooks?
Visit www.millsandboon.co.uk

To the town of Malanda, which doesn't need saving,
and to Deb Healy at the bakery for showing me
how beautiful bread is created every day.

CHAPTER ONE

Boutique business opportunity at Bellaroo Creek

Former bakery offered at nominal or deferred rental to help revitalise the town's retail business.

Bellaroo Council, in support of the Regional Recovery Programme, is calling for expressions of interest to occupy and redevelop Lot 3 Wattle Street on a lease or freehold arrangement. Some bakery equipment is included in the assets.

Enquiries/business plan to J. P. Elliot CEO Bellaroo Council, 23 Wattle Street.

MILLA SAT ON the edge of the hospital bed, a cup of tea and sandwich untouched beside her.

It was over. She'd lost her baby, and any minute now the nice nurse would pop back to tell her she was free to go.

Go where? Back to the lonely motel room?

From down the hospital corridor the sounds of laughter drifted, along with the happy chatter of cheery visitors. Other patients' visitors. Milla looked around her room, bare of cards or flowers, grapes or teddy bears.

Her parents were away on a Mediterranean cruise and she hadn't told anyone else that she was back in Australia.

Her Aussie friends still thought she was living the high life as the wife of a mega-rich Californian and she hadn't been ready to confess the truth about her spectacularly failed marriage. Besides, the few of her friends who lived in Sydney were party girls, and, being pregnant, Milla hadn't been in party mode. She'd been waiting till the next scan to announce the news about her baby.

But now...

Milla wrapped her arms over her stomach, reliving the cramping pains and terror that had brought her to the emergency ward. She had wept as the doctor examined her, and she'd sobbed helplessly when he told her that she was having a miscarriage. She'd cried for the little lost life, for her lost dreams.

Her marriage fiasco had shattered her hopes of ever finding love and trust in an adult relationship and she'd pinned everything on the promise of a soft, warm baby to hold. She longed for the special bond and unconditional love that only a baby could bring, and she'd been desperate to make a success of motherhood.

Such wonderful dreams she'd nurtured for her little boy or girl, and imagining the months ahead had been so much fun.

Along with watching a tiny, new human being discover the world, Milla had looked forward to patiently caring for her little one. Chances were, it would be a boy—the Cavanaugh wives always seemed to produce sons—and Milla had imagined bathing her little fellow, feeding him, dressing him in sweet little striped sleep-suits, coping with his colic and teething pains and the inevitable sleepless nights.

She'd pictured trips to the park and to the beach as he grew, had even seen herself making his first birthday cake with a cute single candle, and issuing invitations to other mums and babes to join in the party.

Now…

'Ten to twenty per cent of known pregnancies end in miscarriage,' the doctor had informed her matter-of-factly.

But Milla could only see this as another failure on top of her failed marriage. After all, if the statistics were turned around, eighty to ninety per cent of pregnancies were absolutely fine. Just as two thirds of marriages were perfectly happy.

The irony was, she'd become pregnant in a last-ditch attempt to save her marriage. When that had proved to be clearly impossible, she'd turned her hopes and ambitions inwards. To her child.

She'd been mega careful with her diet, taking all the right vitamins and folates, and, although she'd been through a great deal of stress and a long flight from LA to Sydney, she'd made sure that her new lifestyle included a healthy balance of rest and exercise and fresh air.

And yet again, she'd failed. Fighting tears, Milla packed her toothbrush and wallet into the carryall she'd hastily filled when she'd left for the hospital.

It was time to go, and after one last look around the small white room she set off down the long hospital corridor.

The final years of her marriage to Harry Cavanaugh

had been grim, but she'd never felt this low…or this lost…as if she'd been cast adrift in a vast and lonely sea.

Fleetingly, she wondered if she should let Harry know about the baby. But why bother? He wouldn't care.

In his midtown Manhattan office, Ed Cavanaugh was absorbed in reading spreadsheets when his PA buzzed that he had an important call. Time was tight and the info on his computer screen was critical. Ed ignored the buzzer and continued scanning the lines of figures.

A minute later, he sensed his PA at the door.

'Mr Cavanaugh?'

Without looking up, Ed raised a silencing hand as he took a note of the figures he'd been hunting. When he was finished, and not a millisecond before, he shot a glance over the top of his glasses. 'What is it, Sarah?'

'A call from Australia. It's Gary Kemp and I was sure you'd want to speak to him.'

Gary Kemp was the Australian private detective Ed's family had had hired to track down his escapee sister-in-law. An unexpected tension gripped Ed. Had Milla been found?

'Put him through,' he said, closing down the screen.

Scant seconds later, his line buzzed again and he snatched up the receiver. 'Gary, any news?'

'Plenty, Mr C.'

'Have you found her? Is she still in Australia?' They already knew that Milla had caught a flight from LA to Sydney.

'She's still in the country, but you'll never guess where.'

Ed grimaced. This Aussie detective could be annoyingly cocky. Ed had no intention of playing guessing games, although in this case it would be dead easy to take a stab at Milla's whereabouts. Her tastes were totally predictable. She would be holed up in a harbour-side penthouse, or in a luxury resort at one of those famous Australian beaches.

'Just tell me,' he demanded with a spurt of irritation.

'Try Bellaroo Creek.'

'Bella-who *what*?'

'Bellaroo Creek,' Gary repeated with a chuckle. 'Middle of nowhere. Dying town. Population three hundred and seventy-nine.'

Ed let out a huff of surprise. 'Where exactly is this middle of nowhere?'

'Little tinpot whistle-stop in western New South Wales, about five hours' drive from Sydney.'

'What are you telling me? My sister-in-law passed through this place?'

'No, she's still there, mate. Seems it's her hometown.'

Just in time, Ed stopped himself from asking the obvious. Of course, his brother's sophisticated socialite wife must have grown up in this Bellaroo Creek place, but he found the news hard to swallow.

'Her family's long gone,' the detective went on. 'So have most of the former residents. As I said, the place is on its last legs. These days it's practically a ghost town.'

None of this made sense to Ed. 'Are you sure you have the right Milla Cavanaugh?'

'No doubt about it. It's her all right, although she's using her maiden name, Brady. Interesting. As far as I can tell, she's barely touched her bank accounts.'

'No way,' retorted Ed. 'You can't have the right woman.'

'Check your emails,' Gary Kemp responded dryly.

'This isn't amateur hour, mate, as you'll soon see from my invoice. I've sent you the photo I took yesterday in Bellaroo Creek's main street.'

Frowning, Ed flicked to his emails, opened the link and there it was…a photo of a woman dressed in jeans and a roll-necked black cashmere sweater.

She was definitely Milla. Her delicate, high-cheek-boned beauty was in a class of its own. His younger brother had always won the best-looking women, no question.

Milla's hair was different, though. Pale red-gold, with a tendency to curl, the way it had been when Ed had first met her, before she'd had it straightened and dyed blond to fit in with the other wives in Harry's LA set.

'OK,' he growled, his throat unaccountably tight. 'That's helpful. I see you've sent an address, as well.'

'Yeah. She's staying at the Bellaroo pub. Booked in for a week, but I'm guessing she might think twice about staying that long. It's so dead here, she could get jack of the place and shoot through any tick of the clock.'

'Right. Thanks for the update. Keep an eye on her and keep me posted re her movements.'

'No worries, Mr C.'

Ed hung up and went through to his PA's desk. 'We've found her.'

Sarah looked unexpectedly delighted. 'That's wonderful, Mr Cavanaugh. Does that mean Milla's still in Australia? Is she OK?'

'Yes on both counts. But it means I'm going to have to fly down there pronto. I'll need you to reschedule the meetings with Cleaver Holdings.'

'Yes, of course.'

'Several people won't be happy, but that's too bad. Dan Brookes will have to handle their complaints and he can run any other meetings in my absence. I'll brief him as soon as he's free. Meantime, I want you to book me on the earliest possible flight to Sydney. And I'll want a hire car ready to go.'

'Of course.'

'And can you ring Caro Marsden? Let her know I'll be out of the country for a few days.'

To his surprise Sarah, his normally respectful PA, narrowed her eyes at him in an uncharacteristic challenge. 'Ed,' she said, which was a bad start. Sarah rarely used his given name. 'You've been dating the poor woman for four months. Don't you think you should—'

'All right, all right,' he snapped through gritted teeth. 'I'll call her.'

Sarah was watching him with a thoughtful frown. 'I guess you're going to break the news to Milla about your brother?'

'Among other things.' Ed eased the sudden tightness of his collar. His younger brother's death in a plane crash and the subsequent funeral were still fresh and raw. The loss had hit him so much harder than he'd imagined possible.

'The poor woman,' Sarah said now.

'Yeah,' Ed responded softly…remembering…and wondering…

Almost immediately, he gave an irritated shrug, annoyed by the unwanted pull of his emotions. 'Don't forget, it was Milla who cut and ran,' he said tersely.

Not only that. She kept her pregnancy a secret from

the family. Which was the prime reason he had to find her now.

'I know Milla's persona non grata around here,' Sarah said. 'But I always thought she seemed very nice.'

Sure you did, Ed thought with a sigh. That was the problem. The woman had always been a total enigma.

It was weird to be back. It had been twelve long years...

Milla drove her little hire car over a bumpy wooden bridge and took the next turn left onto a dirt track. As she opened the farm gates she saw a large rustic letter-box with the owners' names—BJ and HA Murray—painted in white.

She hadn't seen her old school friends, Brad and Heidi, since she'd left town when she was twenty, dead eager to shake the district's dust from her heels and to travel the world. Back then, she'd been determined to broaden her horizons and to discover her hidden potential, to work out what she really wanted from life.

Meanwhile Heidi, her best friend, had stayed here in this quiet old backwater. Worse, Heidi had made the deadly serious mistake of marrying a local boy, an error of judgement the girls had decreed in high school would be a fate worse than death.

Shoot me now, they used to say at the very thought. They'd been sixteen then. Sixteen and super confident that the world was their oyster, and quite certain that it was vitally important to escape Bellaroo Creek.

Unfortunately, Heidi had changed her mind and she'd become engaged to Brad only a matter of months after Milla had left town.

But although poor old Heidi had stayed, it was clear

that many others had found it necessary to get away. These days Bellaroo Creek was practically a ghost town.

This discovery had been a bit of a shock. Milla had hoped that a trip to her hometown would cheer her up. Instead, she'd been depressed all over again when she'd walked down the main street and discovered that almost all the businesses and shops had closed down.

Where were the cars and people? Where were the farmers standing on street corners, thumbs hooked in belt loops as they discussed the weather and the wool prices? Where were the youngsters who used to hang around the bakery or the hamburger joint? The young mums who brought their babies to the clinic, their children to the library?

Bellaroo Creek was nothing like the busy, friendly country town of her childhood. The general store was now a supermarket combined with a newsagent's and a tiny post office—and that was just about it.

Even the bakery Milla's parents used to own was now boarded-up and empty. Milla had stood for ages outside the shopfront she'd once known so well, staring glumly through the dusty, grimy windows into the darkened interior.

From as far back as she could remember the Bellaroo bakery had been a bustling, busy place, filled with cheery customers, and with the fragrant aroma of freshly baked bread. People had flocked from miles around to buy her dad's mouth-watering loaves made from local wheat, or his delicious rolls and shiny-topped fruit buns, as well as her mum's legendary pies.

Her parents had sold the business when they retired, and in the short time since it had come to this…an empty, grimy shop with a faded, printed sign inside the dusty window offering the place for lease. Again.

Who would want it?

Looking around at the other vacant shopfronts, Milla had been totally disheartened. She'd driven from Sydney to Bellaroo Creek on a nostalgic whim, but instead she'd found a place on the brink of extinction...

It seemed the universe was presenting her with yet another dismal picture of failure.

It was so depressing...

Poor Heidi must be going mental living here, Milla decided as she drove down the winding dirt track between paddocks of pale, biscuit-coloured grass dotted with fat, creamy sheep. At least Heidi was still married to Brad and had two kids, a boy and a girl—which sounded fine on the surface, but Milla couldn't believe her old friend was really happy.

Admittedly, her contact with Heidi had been patchy— the occasional email or Facebook message, the odd Christmas card...

She'd felt quite tentative, almost fearful when she'd plucked up the courage to telephone Heidi, and she'd been rather surprised that her friend had sounded just as bright and bubbly as she had in her teens.

'Come for lunch,' Heidi had gushed after the initial excited squeal over the phone. 'Better still, come for morning tea and stay for lunch. That way you'll catch up with Brad when he comes in around twelve, and we can have plenty of time for a really good chat. I want to hear *everything.*'

Milla wasn't particularly looking forward to sharing too many details of her personal history, but she was keen to see Heidi again. Curious now, too, as the track dipped to a concrete ford that crossed a small, shady creek.

As her tyres splashed through the shallow water she imagined Heidi and Brad's children playing in the creek when they were older. She edged the car up the opposite bank and rounded a corner, and saw her first view of the farmhouse.

Which wasn't grand by any means—just a simple white weatherboard house with verandahs and a red roof—but it was shaded by a big old spreading tree and there were well-tended flowerbeds set in neat lawns, a vegetable garden with trellises at one end and free-ranging, rusty-feathered chickens.

Her friend's home was a far cry from the acres of expensive glass and white marble of Milla and Harry's Beverly Hills mansion…

And yet, something about the house's old-fashioned, rustic simplicity touched an unexpected chord in Milla.

No need to get sentimental, she warned herself as she drove forward.

Before she'd parked the car, the front door opened, spilling puppies and a rosy-cheeked little girl. Heidi followed close behind, waving and grinning as she hurried down the steps and across the lawn. As Milla clambered out she found herself enveloped in the warmest of welcoming hugs.

After weeks of loneliness, she was fighting tears.

Ed had tried to ring his father several times, but the arrogant old man had a habit of ignoring phone calls if he wasn't in a sociable mood. Which happened quite often, and went part-way to explaining Gerry Cavanaugh's multiple marriages and divorces and why his three sons had been born to three different wives, who now lived as far apart from each other as possible.

Today, when Gerry finally deigned to return his son's call, Ed was in the Business Lounge at JFK, sending last-minute business emails.

'Glad to hear you've tracked Milla down.' His father always jumped in without any preliminaries. 'And you know what you have to do when you catch up with her, don't you, Ed?'

'Well…sure. I'll tell her about Harry.'

'If she doesn't already know.'

Ed was quite sure Milla couldn't know that Harry had died. Even though she'd run away, she would have been upset. She would have contacted them if she'd heard, and come back for the funeral.

'And I'll set up the trust fund for the baby,' he went on. 'Make sure Milla signs the necessary papers.'

'That's not all, damn it.'

Ed sighed. What else had his old man up his sleeve?

'Your main job is to bring the woman home.'

'Home?' This was news to Ed. 'Don't forget Milla was born and bred in Australia, Father. And she still calls Australia home,' he added with a grim smile at his joking reference to the popular song.

'Like hell. My grandson will be born in America.'

'What are you suggesting? That I kidnap a pregnant woman? You want extradition orders placed on your pregnant daughter-in-law?'

His father ignored this. 'You'll find a way to persuade her. You're a Cavanaugh. You have a knack with women.'

Not with this particular woman. Ed squashed unsettling memories before they could take hold. 'Just remember, Father. Milla ran away from Harry and from our family. It's obvious she wants as much distance between us as possible. She's unlikely to come back willingly.'

'Trust me, son, as soon as she hears she's a widow, she'll be back here in a flash. Of course, she won't get a goddamn cent of Harry's money unless she lets us raise the child as a Cavanaugh, as my grandchild.'

'Got it...' responded Ed dispiritedly. 'I'll see what I can do.'

His offer was received with an expressive grunt that conveyed the full brunt of his father's doubts and displeasure.

Ed gritted his teeth. 'Anyway...I've briefed Dan Brookes and everything's in hand as far as the business is concerned, so I guess I'll see you in a couple of days.'

Ending the call, Ed sat staring bleakly through the wall of windows, watching the busy tarmac and the endless streams of planes taking off and landing.

He wasn't looking forward to the long, twenty-hour flight, but he was looking forward even less to the task that lay ahead of him. After all, Milla had returned to Australia because she'd planned to divorce Harry, and she'd clearly been so disenchanted with the Cavanaughs that she hadn't told them about her pregnancy.

It was only while Ed and his father were going through the painful process of sorting through Harry's paperwork that they'd discovered the medical forms.

Slam!

A small missile crashed into Ed, sending his Black-Berry flying. Rascal-faced yet cherubic, a little boy looked up at him with enormous and cheeky blue eyes that peeped from beneath a white-blond fringe.

'What's your name?' the kid lisped cutely as he gripped at Ed's trouser leg for balance.

'Ethan!' A woman dived from the right, sweeping the child into her arms. 'So sorry,' she told Ed, her eyes widening with horror as she saw her son's sticky, chocolate-smeared fingers and the tracks he'd left on Ed's Italian suit trousers.

The kid squirmed in his mom's arms, as if he sensed that his fun was about to end. And Ed couldn't help remembering Harry as an ankle-biter.

For ages after the woman and her boy disappeared, Ed sat, thinking about his younger brother. Milla's unborn baby would probably be just like that kid—an angelic rascal, full of mischief and charm, stealing hearts and creating havoc. Another Cavanaugh…a new generation.

Memories washed over him as they had many times in the past few weeks. Growing up with different mothers, he and Harry hadn't spent a lot of time in each other's company, but his younger brother had always been the wild child, the prankster, the kid who hadn't done his homework, but still passed his exams with good grades.

As an adult, Harry had wasted his talents on gambling and flying his private jet and he'd contributed almost nothing to the family firm. And yet, they'd all loved him. Despite his faults, the guy had been a born charmer.

Ed was the conscientious son, the hardworking eldest, the one who'd carried on the family's business so that all the others could continue to live in the manner to which they'd become accustomed.

Admittedly, their youngest brother, Charlie, the son

of Gerry Cavanaugh's third wife, was still in college. He was a good student, from all reports, more serious and focused, more like Ed. But they'd both known that Harry had always been the Golden Child, their father's favourite, and Harry's son would be the apple of his grandfather's eye.

Ed would have to deal with the full force of his father's wrath if he failed to bring Milla and her unborn baby home.

Sitting at Heidi's scrubbed pine table, drinking coffee and talking nineteen to the dozen, Milla made a surprising discovery. She felt calmer and happier than she had in...ages...

Looking around at Heidi's honey-toned timber cupboards and simple open shelving, at the jars of home-made preserves and pots of herbs on the window sill, she realised that she'd completely forgotten how very comforting a farmhouse kitchen could be.

This room had such a timeless and welcoming quality with its huge old stove pumping out gentle warmth, with Heidi's home-baked cookies on a willow-pattern plate...a yellow jug filled with bottlebrush flowers... dog and cat bowls in the corner...

It brought to mind Milla's childhood here in Bellaroo Creek. She'd been happy back then.

Chatting with Heidi was so very different from socialising in LA, where the women's conversations had been more like competitions, and the topics centred on shopping, facials, pedicures, or gossip about affairs.

Heidi simply talked about her family, who were clearly the centre of her world. She told Milla about Brad's farming innovations with the same pride she displayed when she mentioned her son's success in his first year at school or her little daughter's playful antics.

The conversation should have been boring, but Milla found to her surprise that she was fascinated.

It was all a bit puzzling... Heidi's hair was still exactly the same as it had been in high school—straight, shoulder length and mousey brown. She spent her days working on the farm with Brad and growing vegetables and raising chickens, which meant she lived in jeans and cotton shirts and sturdy boots.

She had freckles and a few lines around her eyes, and her hands were roughened, her fingernails chipped. But Milla, looking at her friend, knew she was as happy as a pig in the proverbial...

'I'm doing exactly what I want to do,' Heidi happily confessed. 'Maybe I'm totally lacking in ambition, but I don't want to do anything else. And it might sound crazy, but I don't have any doubts.'

This was a *major* surprise, but to her even greater surprise Milla found herself opening up to Heidi telling how she'd clocked many, many miles and tried a ton of different jobs in exotic locations, until eventually, she'd arrived in America and fallen head over heels for a charming and handsome multimillionaire adventurer, who had, incredibly, asked her to marry him.

She told how those first years of her marriage had been such a heady time. Harry had so many celebrity friends in his social circle and he'd flown his own plane. 'He used to fly me to Paris for a dinner and a show, or to Milan to buy a dress I could wear to the Oscars.'

Heidi's jaw dropped with a satisfying clunk.

'We would fly to New Orleans for a party,' Milla went on. 'Or to Buenos Aires to watch a polo game. I never dreamed I'd ever have such excitement and fun, such astonishing luxury and comfort.'

'I used to hear bits and pieces,' Heidi said, overawed. 'But I never realised you were living like a princess. Wow! It must have been *amazing*.'

'Yeah.' Milla wished she could sound more convincing. She couldn't quite bring herself to tell Heidi the rest of her story—about Harry's gambling and endless affairs, and if she mentioned the baby she would burst into tears.

Crazy thing was, she'd come back to Bellaroo Creek full of pity for Heidi, but, looking back on her own life, she felt as if she'd achieved next to nothing that really counted. In terms of happiness and self-esteem, she was at an all-time low.

And it wasn't long before she sensed that her friend had guessed. She could see the questions and the dawning compassion in Heidi's eyes. And then, out of the blue, as if they'd never lost their best-friends-for-ever closeness, Heidi jumped out of her chair, circled the table and gave Milla an enormous hug.

'Mills, you have to tell me why you're here on your own and looking so sad,' Heidi said gently. 'And what are we going to do about it?'

CHAPTER TWO

At last…a road sign announced: *Welcome to Bellaroo Creek… Population 379…*

Ed slowed the car and surveyed the cluster of tired houses and the narrow strip of faded office buildings and shops set in the middle of wide, almost feature-less plains. It was like arriving on the set of a West-ern movie. And potentially as risky, he thought wryly.

A new tension replaced his frayed and jet-lagged weariness as he pulled over, took out his phone and punched Gary Kemp's number. He'd given Milla no warning of his arrival—he'd more or less come here to ambush her. It wasn't a pleasant prospect.

'Mr Cavanaugh,' the Australian drawled, recognis-ing Ed's number. 'Welcome to Oz.'

More like Kansas than Oz, Ed almost told him. 'Milla still here?' he asked. 'Still staying at the pub?'

'Sure, her room's booked through till Wednesday and she's still in town, but you're more likely to find her in the old bakery across the road.'

Ed frowned. He'd heard of pregnant women develop-ing food cravings, but he couldn't imagine his slender sister-in-law wolfing down endless strudels.

'Apparently her family used to own the bakery,' Gary

Kemp clarified. 'It's closed now, but she seems to have the keys.'

'OK, that's helpful.' Ed scratched at his jaw, finding a patch of stubble he'd missed during his hasty shave at Sydney airport. 'I'll take it from here.'

'Glad to hear it, Mr C. I certainly don't want to hang around in this hole any longer than I have to. It's probably safer if you and I don't meet. I've just fuelled up on the other side of town, so I'll head off.'

'So the bakery's easy to find?'

'Can't miss it. In the main street, opposite the pub and about three doors along.'

'Thanks.' Ed edged his car forward, cruising into the almost deserted main street where a few battered pickup trucks and dusty sedans were parked. A couple of pedestrians crossed the road at a shuffling snail's pace—a young woman, arm in arm with an elderly, white-haired man huddled inside a tweed jacket.

Further down the street, two women holding laden shopping bags were deep in conversation. A spotted dog slept in a sunny doorway.

Otherwise, the street appeared empty, but despite the lack of people the town didn't look completely neglected. A neat and colourful strip of garden cut the wide street in half, clear evidence that someone cared. There were shade trees, too, and noisy, brightly coloured birds were feeding in the blossom-filled branches.

The taller buildings were no higher than two storeys, but they looked solid and stately and over a century old, signs to Ed that the town had seen better days. Opposite the post office a memorial had been erected to fallen soldiers and there seemed to be a hell of a lot of names on it.

Bellaroo Creek had boasted a bigger population at one time, he decided as he parked a few doors away from the pub and took off his sunglasses, conscious again of his tiredness after the long flight and the five-hour drive on the wrong side of the highway.

Tension nagged and he grimaced. He wasn't looking forward to the task ahead.

He told himself he was doing it for the kid's sake. Now, with Harry gone, Ed's role as the unborn baby's uncle loomed as a greater responsibility, with higher personal stakes. He would cope best if he concentrated on the kid and erased from his memory his fleeting history with its mother.

Frowning, he climbed out of the car and stretched his long, cramped limbs. Across the road, he could see a row of rundown, empty shopfronts in stone buildings that still showed traces of their former elegance. One door was open and above it, in faded green paint, the shop's name, Bellaroo Bakery, was faintly visible.

With an air of determination Ed crossed the road and stood on the sidewalk outside, observing. He couldn't see anyone in the front part of the store, but he listened for voices. Although he planned to take Milla by surprise, he didn't want to embarrass her if she had company.

There was silence, however, so he knocked on the open door.

And waited impatiently.

No one came and he was about to knock again when Milla appeared at the back of the shop, wiping her hands on her jeans. She looked pale and tired, but her delicate features and candle-flame hair were as lovely as ever. And, as always, the sight of her sent a painful dart spearing through Ed.

Her face turned white when she saw him.

'You?' she said softly and her sea-green eyes looked stricken. Her lips trembled, parted and then shut again as if she couldn't think of anything else to say.

Ed swallowed to ease the sharpness in his throat and Milla came forward carefully, almost fearfully.

'Hello, Milla.'

'What are you doing here?'

'I—' He was halted by her fragile air, suddenly afraid that his news would flatten her completely. 'There've been…developments.' *Damn, how clumsy was that?* 'We need to talk.'

'No, thanks.' Green fire flared in Milla's eyes. 'I'm finished with you lot.' She shot him a tight, haughty glare. 'I have nothing to discuss with you or with your brother.'

Turning away, she tossed her next words over her shoulder. 'I know why you're here, Ed. Harry sent you, because he didn't have the guts to come and try to con me himself. But I don't care if he wants me back. I'm done with him. It's over.'

'Harry didn't ask me to come.'

Milla stiffened, half turned towards him again. Her eyes were sharp, her arms crossed defensively over her chest. 'How did you find me?' Before Ed could answer, a knowing light crept into her eyes. 'It was that weasel-faced guy in the pub, wasn't it? He's watching me. He's a private investigator.'

Ed shrugged.

'Cavanaugh money,' she scoffed bitterly. 'It'll buy anything.'

'Milla, I've come a long way and we need to—'

'You shouldn't have bothered, Ed. I know your role in the family. Mr Fix-it. The others are always getting you to clean up after them and to sort everyone's problems.'

At least her voice wasn't quite as harsh as she said this.

And Ed found himself fumbling to explain. 'Well… listen…I had to find you. I knew you couldn't know what's happened.'

She frowned. 'What do you mean?'

'Milla, it's bad news about Harry.'

'Harry's always bad news.' Now she gave a theatrical eye-roll, as if she hadn't heard the seriousness in his voice. 'It took me four years to discover what you and your family probably knew all along.'

'Milla, Harry's dead.'

To Ed's dismay Milla's face turned whiter than ever. She clamped a hand to her mouth and she seemed to crumple and sway.

Instinctively, he stepped forward. The reaction was timely as Milla sagged against him as if her knees had given way.

Horrified, Ed remembered too late that she was pregnant. He should have delivered the news more gently, instead of oafishly blurting it out.

Scooping her into his arms, he scanned the empty shop, but there wasn't so much as a chair. He carried her, trying, unsuccessfully, to ignore her soft curves and the flowery fragrance of her hair. Through the doorway, and at the back of the shop he found a huge cleaned space with, among other things, a scrubbed table and chairs. But already, Milla was stirring.

* * *

'I'm sorry.'

Milla realised she was being carried in Ed's arms with her face pressed against the solid wall of his chest. 'I'm OK, Ed,' she protested, although she was still feeling dizzy. 'Put me down, please.'

He was incredibly gentle as he lowered her to a chair. 'Are you sure you're OK?'

'Yes, thank you.' It wasn't completely true. She was still dazed by the news.

Harry couldn't be dead. It was impossible. She felt sick and faint and she propped her elbows on the table and sank her head in her hands, trying to take the astonishing news in.

Her husband was dead. The man who'd caused her so much initial joy and subsequent pain. Desperately handsome, dangerously charming, hurtful and selfish Harry Cavanaugh. Gone. For ever.

When she'd left America she'd hated him. He'd lied and cheated on her one time too many, and in the worst possible way. In his final act of faithlessness, she'd come home unexpectedly early from an appointment with her obstetrician and found him in bed—*their* bed—with one of her so-called girlfriends.

It wasn't the first time and Milla knew she'd been foolish to forgive him in the past. Leaving Harry had been easy after that.

But now…

Death.

No chance for forgiveness either way.

Milla was aware that Ed had moved to the sink and was filling a glass with water.

'Thanks,' she said as he offered her the drink. She took a few small sips.

'Milla, I'm sorry. I should have been more thought-ful—'

'There's no thoughtful way to break this kind of news. I made it difficult to be found, so it was good of you to come, Ed, to tell me face to face.' She took another sip of water and forced herself to ask, 'What happened? How did Harry—?' But she couldn't bring herself to say the dreadful word. 'How did it happen?'

'He crashed his plane.'

'No.' Milla flinched as she pictured the beautiful sleek and shiny jet—Harry's pride and joy—crumpled. Burned. Harry inside.

'It happened over the Mojave Desert,' Ed said. 'The funeral was last Thursday.'

It was the same day she'd lost the baby. Remember-ing, she was so overwhelmed she had to cover her face with her hands. Sinking forward, she compressed her lips tightly to stop herself from sobbing out loud.

By the time she was once again under control, Ed was at the side window, standing with his back to her and with his hands plunged deep in his trouser pockets as he looked out into the untidy, narrow alley between this shop and its neighbour.

'I would have come back to the funeral,' she said.

Ed nodded. 'I knew you would have, but we couldn't find you.'

'I'm sorry.' She was. Truly sorry. Despite the many times Harry had hurt her, she still felt something for him, although she wasn't quite sure what that some-thing was.

'Was there anyone else in the plane?'

A muscle jerked in Ed's jaw. 'Yes.'

'Not Julie?'

'No,' Ed said wearily. 'Julie had already been passed over.' He looked down at the floor and his throat worked as he swallowed, as if he hated what he had to tell her next. 'It was Angela.'

A groan broke from Milla. 'Angela Beldon?'

'Yes,' Ed said unhappily.

Another from her circle of so-called friends…

Harry, you poor silly man…

'It must be genetic, don't you think?'

'What's that?'

'The Cavanaugh male's wandering eye.'

Ed frowned. 'You're probably right.' He sighed and turned back to the window, as if he hoped this difficult conversation had come to an end.

He was every inch a Cavanaugh, with the family's typically strong features and broad-shouldered muscularity. An inch or two taller than Harry, he was as dark as his younger brother had been fair, but, like the rest of the family, he had an indefinable masculine ruggedness that inevitably drew admiring glances from women.

That was where the similarities ended, however. Ed was the serious, responsible member of the Cavanaugh clan. *The Good Son,* Harry had dubbed him, but, while Harry's tone had been mocking, there'd been a hint of envy, too.

Milla, for her part, had always been a little in awe of Ed, even a bit afraid of him.

She was nervous now, realising that there had to be more to his sudden arrival in Bellaroo Creek than the delivery of bad news that could have been handled— now that they'd tracked her down—with a phone call.

'I suppose you came all this way to talk about money,' she said dully.

Ed turned from the window. 'It has to be discussed. Apart from anything else, we have to settle your inheritance.'

She shook hear head.

'As I'm sure you know,' Ed went on, 'my father placed certain restrictions on Harry. He made sure it was in your pre-nup.'

Yes, Milla knew that Gerry Cavanaugh had learned hard lessons after being royally screwed by three wives. She had no intention of completing that pattern. 'I don't want Harry's money.'

Ed narrowed his smoky grey eyes as he studied her for long thoughtful seconds. Then he shrugged. 'I know you gave up your right to the money when you left the marriage, but now that Harry's...' He swallowed unhappily. 'Now that he's...gone...you still have a claim as his widow.'

'I said, I don't want any of it, Ed.' She was determined to manage on her own and she didn't want money from anyone—not even her own parents, who would have happily helped her out if she'd let them. For now, she was pleased that her mother and father were safely overseas and unaware of her plans.

Ed's eyes widened as he stared at her, clearly taken aback by her claim. 'Maybe it's too soon for you to think about this.'

Milla felt a stirring of impatience. She wasn't playing games. She was deadly serious. She still had some money in her bank accounts and that was all she wanted.

Most women would think she was crazy to knock back a fortune, and if she'd still had her baby to consider her reaction might have been different. But her take-home lesson from her marriage was that even Himalayan-sized mountains of money couldn't buy the things that really mattered.

Sure, money bought power and glamour and ease and moments of heady excitement, but in her four years of marriage and rubbing shoulders with the mega wealthy she'd never seen evidence that these things added up to genuine, lasting happiness.

She only had to remember Heidi's bone-deep contentment with her seemingly 'boring' life to reinforce this belief.

'If you come back to the States,' Ed said, breaking into her thoughts, 'you and the baby will be much better off.'

Shocked, she looked up swiftly. 'You know about the—about my pregnancy?'

'Yes,' he said gently. 'It's wonderful news.'

So Harry had told them, after all…

'That's why you've come, isn't it? Old Gerry sent you. He wants his grandchild to live in America.'

'It's understandable, Milla.'

'It's not going to happen.'

'Look, I'm sure you need a little time to think this through.'

'It's not a matter of time. There's no baby, Ed.'

'What do you mean? What are you saying?'

Her voice quavered. 'I lost it. I had a miscarriage.'

He looked shocked. 'No.'

'It's the truth,' she said tightly, but she saw doubt and suspicion in his storm-cloud eyes and realised, to her horror, that he wasn't going to believe her.

Damn him.

He was pacing now, clearly baffled and probably angry.

'Ed, this isn't something I'd lie about. I was in a hospital, not an abortion clinic. I really wanted my baby.' Her lips trembled and she drew a sharp breath, but she was determined that she wouldn't dissolve into tears. The fainting spell had been bad enough. She had to be strong to stand up to this man.

'If you don't believe me, get that PI you hired to check out the RPA Hospital. I'm sure he'll be able to ferret out the proof you need.'

'Milla, don't be like that.'

'Don't be like *what*?' Her voice was shrill, but that was too bad. 'I'll give you *don't*. Don't you dare look at me like I'm lying about something that meant everything to me.'

Now she was so mad and upset she was shaking.

'OK, I apologise.' He stood before her, with his hands once again in his jeans pockets, his shoulders squared, his jaw tight, his eyes a battlefield where doubt and sympathy warred.

It was late afternoon and a wintry chill made Milla shiver. Shadows crept across the thick stone sill of the bakery window and spread along the brick walls and the ancient and worn stone floor. In the fading light, she could see that Ed looked deeply tired.

He'd had a long journey from New York and he'd probably driven straight from the airport. He had to be dead on his feet.

'I'm sorry about the baby,' he said quietly.

'I'm sorry you came all this way for nothing.'

The slightest hint of a smile flickered, giving a cynical tilt to his lips, but his eyes continued to regard her solemnly.

It was so not the right moment to remember the one time he'd kissed her. But the memory came, unbidden, bringing rivers of heat rushing under her clothes.

'Maybe we can have a more civilised discussion about everything over dinner,' he suggested.

'There's nothing to discuss.'

'Milla, I'm not the Cavanaugh who stuffed up your life. Surely we can share a meal before I go back.'

Perhaps she *was* overreacting. 'I guess. But there's really only one place in town to eat and that's the pub.'

'I'll need to check in to the hotel. You're still staying there, aren't you?'

Milla nodded. 'Until I get this place cleaned up.'

'This place?' Frowning, Ed looked around the bakery as if he was seeing it for the first time. His steely gaze took in the metal tables, the big gas cooker, the trolleys and baking trays and bins, the massive oven that filled the far wall. Finally, his gaze rested on the brooms and mop and bucket in the corner. 'Are you having the bakery cleaned?'

'In a manner of speaking—except I'm the one doing the cleaning.'

This time, Ed didn't even try to hide his disbelief.

'I'm not only *cleaning* the bakery. I plan to get it up and running again.' Before he could comment, Milla hurried to explain. 'The former owners went broke, along with several other businesses here, and the local council is offering peppercorn rent for people willing to restart. I've put in an application for this bakery and, as far as I know, no one else is interested.'

'I'm not surprised,' he muttered, just loud enough

for her to hear. 'One question.' He stared at her again. 'Why?'

'My family used to own this bakery. I know how to run a place like this. I grew up here.'

Still, Ed looked puzzled. 'So?'

Milla sighed. How did she explain everything she'd seen and felt since her arrival in Bellaroo Creek? How could she explain her longing to do something meaningful after years of unfulfilling luxury and wastefulness?

This billionaire standing before her in his high-end designer-label jeans and polo shirt couldn't possibly understand how the resurrection of this humble country bakery was an important chance to do something positive, not just for herself, but for a whole community.

'The town needs help, Ed. Bellaroo Creek is on the brink of extinction, but a local committee has started a plan to rescue it. Everything hinges on keeping the school open, so they're inviting families to rent farmhouses for a dollar a week.'

'Desperate families.'

'People who want to make a new start,' Milla defended. 'People looking for fresh air and something better than a dark backstreet alley for their kids to play in. A place where people know each other by name and have a sense of community.'

'You've been brainwashed, haven't you?'

'I'm looking for a way of life that makes me feel fulfilled,' she said hotly. 'And this is something I'm determined to do without touching my ex's money.'

His mouth tightened. 'It's a knee-jerk reaction, Milla. You're not being rational.'

'I'm not asking for your approval, Ed.'

'Look, I said I'm sorry about the baby, and I am, honestly, more than you can guess. And hell, I'm sorry your marriage to my brother didn't work out—but I know business and commerce inside out, and I know for absolute certainty that you'll regret this.'

'I really don't want to fight about it,' she said firmly but decisively.

After all, what she did with her life now was *her* business. The Cavanaughs no longer had any kind of hold on her.

However, Ed had no choice but to stay in Bellaroo Creek tonight and the pub was his only accommodation option. 'As you said, we can try for a civilised conversation over dinner.'

'I'm glad you agree.'

'At least we won't be able to yell at each other in the pub dining room.'

'That's a relief.'

'The chef is Chinese,' Milla told him. 'And he's pretty good. I think you'll like his duck with mushrooms.'

Ed's eyebrows lifted and, at last, there was a hint of a smile. 'Duck with mushrooms way out here?'

'Bellaroo Creek has one or two surprises.'

'OK. Sounds good.' He pulled his cell phone from his pocket and noted the time. 'I need to check in.'

It was, at best, a temporary truce, but Milla let out a huff of relief.

'I'll come with you,' she said. 'Unfortunately, Sherry, the girl on the reception desk, isn't as professional as the chef. There are so few people who check in here, she often wanders off to help in the kitchen or the laundry. Sometimes you have to go hunting for her.'

* * *

Five minutes later, having checked the pub's bar, the lounge, the dining room, the laundry and the kitchen without unearthing Sherry, Milla returned to Reception to find Ed in a spindly wooden chair with his eyes shut and his long legs stretched in front of him. He seemed to be asleep, although he looked dreadfully uncomfortable.

'Ed.' She touched his knee and he woke with a start. 'I can't find the reception girl and you look like you need to sleep.'

'I'm fine,' he insisted, blinking and frowning as he got to his feet.

'You're exhausted and jet lagged. I think you should come up to my room.' To her annoyance she felt a bright blush as she said this. 'You can at least have a shower while I track down someone who can organise a room for you,' she went on brusquely.

'A shower sounds good.' Ed yawned. 'Thanks, I won't say no.'

The offer of her room had seemed practical and sensible to Milla until she climbed the narrow staircase with Ed beside her. In the confined space she was super aware of his height and broad shoulders and mega-masculine aura. Her heartbeats picked up pace and her skin prickled and even her breathing seemed to falter.

By the time they reached her room she was ridiculously flustered. When she pushed the door open, she took a necessary step back. 'After you, Ed.'

'Thanks.' He set his expensive leather duffle bag on the floor and stood with his hands propped on his hips, surveying her double bed and the cosmetics scattered over the old-fashioned dressing table, the wardrobe with an oval, age-spotted mirror on the door.

'It's old-fashioned but at least there's an en-suite. The bathroom's through here.' She moved to the louvre doors, newly painted white, and pushed them open. 'It's tiny, but adequate. There's a spare towel on the shelf above the—'

Oh, help.

Why hadn't she remembered that she'd left her undies hanging above the bath? Now her silky panties and lacy bras were on full display. To make matters worse, rosy light from the setting sun streamed through the high bathroom window, gilding the lingerie's creamy fragility.

And Ed was smiling. 'Nice decor,' he said with a grin. But a darker glint in his eyes lit flames inside Milla.

Leaping forward, she hastily grabbed the offending articles, bunching them into a tight ball. If she'd had a pocket she would have shoved them into it.

She kept her gaze safely lowered. 'The bathroom's all yours.'

CHAPTER THREE

ED WAS COLD. As he clambered from a black hole of deep, drugging sleep he opened his eyes a chink and discovered chill grey dawn light filling a strange room. Everything was alien—the shapes of the furniture, the position of the windows.

He had no idea where he was.

And he was cold. Naked and cold. Instinctively, he groped for the bed covers, and as he lifted them he caught a drift of flowery scent. With a jolt of dismay, he remembered Milla.

This was Australia. He was in a hotel in Bellaroo Creek. He'd showered in Milla's bathroom. This was her bedroom.

They were supposed to have had dinner together.

Where was she?

Shivering, he rolled under the covers, relishing the new-found warmth as his mind struggled to sort out his dilemma. Or rather, Milla's dilemma. It was obvious now that he'd come out of the shower last night, seen her bed, and fallen onto it in exhaustion.

With that part of the puzzle sorted, he could all too easily picture the rest. Milla had come back to her room to find him sprawled, naked, on her bed. Out like a light.

No doubt she'd bolted like a frightened squirrel, and he could only hope the hotel people had given her another room, the room that should have been his.

What a stuff-up. Now he would have to start the day with apologies. Never a comfortable exercise.

Groaning, Ed burrowed deeper under the covers, but already the room was growing lighter and he was all too acutely aware that this was Milla's bed. Although the sheets had probably been changed, the floral perfume he always associated with her lingered. Unhelpfully, he also remembered the delicate wisps of her lingerie that had hung over her bath, and, *man*, that was *not* a useful memory for a red-blooded male at this hour of the morning.

One thing was certain. He wouldn't be getting back to sleep.

'Good morning. You're up bright and early.' A leggy blonde in a cowgirl shirt and jeans grinned broadly at Ed as he walked into the hotel dining room. 'I'm Sherry,' she told him brightly. 'And you're our first customer for breakfast. You're welcome to sit anywhere you like.'

Ed, freshly showered, shaved and changed into clean clothes, chose a small table by a window with a view down Bellaroo Creek's empty and silent main street. In a far corner, a wood fire burned in a grate, making the room cosy, despite its emptiness.

'Would you like tea or coffee to begin with?' Sherry asked.

'Coffee, thanks.'

'Oh, you're American,' she gushed. 'Of course you'll want coffee.' But instead of leaving to fetch a coffeepot, she stood beaming at him.

Ed realised she was the elusive girl Milla had searched for last night, but he wasn't inclined to be talkative first thing in the morning, so he made no comment.

'You're not a movie star, or anything exciting, are you?' she asked next.

'Not the slightest bit exciting,' he replied dryly. 'And I'll have scrambled eggs as well as coffee.' He didn't return her smile.

'With bacon and tomatoes?'

'That'd be great.'

'Sausages?'

'Yes, the lot.' He'd skipped lunch and dinner and he was ravenous enough to eat an entire rhinoceros. 'And I'd like toast and orange juice.'

'Right away, sir. I'll get Stu straight onto it.'

She was back quite soon with a steaming pot and, to Ed's relief, the coffee was strong and hot. He considered asking her about Milla's whereabouts, but opted for discretion.

'You can leave that pot here,' he told her.

He was on his second cup when she came back with a laden breakfast plate. His stomach growled gratefully.

'So you're a friend of Milla's?' she asked coyly, remaining by his table as he tucked into his food.

Ed nodded as he ate, but he had no intention of sharing details of his exact relationship to Milla with this nosy girl.

'We're all excited about Milla starting up the bakery,' the girl said next.

This time he looked up, unable to hide his interest. 'So the town really wants a bakery?'

'Of course. It'll be wonderful. But the problem is, bakeries are so much hard work. Poor Milla will have to work dreadful hours. She'll be up at something like three in the morning.' The girl gave a wide-eyed shake of her head. 'Half the town are right behind her and can't wait for her shop to open. The other half think she's crazy trying to do it on her own. They're betting she'll last a month at the most.'

Ed accepted this news grimly, but he didn't encourage further discussion.

'Mind you, I'm amazed Milla bothered to come back,' said Sherry. 'I mean, with her looks, why would she bury herself here?'

Exactly, thought Ed.

By the time he'd finished his breakfast, there were still no other diners, and no sign of the girl who'd served him. He left her a tip and went out into the street, staring across at the bakery and wondering when Milla would show up.

The other half think she's crazy.

Deep in thought, he crossed the road. The scent of wood smoke lingered in the chilly morning air, reminding him, briefly, of visits to his grandparents' farm in Michigan, but he turned his focus to the bakery.

Yesterday, he'd paid next to no attention to it. He'd been preoccupied with his original mission to persuade Milla to return to the States, and then he'd been side-swiped by her news about the baby. Now, he thought about her plan to set up a business here. This ex Beverly Hills heiress wanted to get up at three in the morning in the middle of winter to bake bread. Not just once, but every day.

Impossible.

Half the good folk of Bellaroo Creek were right. Milla *was* crazy. Running a bakery was damn hard work. Intensely physical labour. Certainly too much for a woman of head-turning beauty who was used to the heights of luxury.

This bakery scheme didn't make any kind of sense. It had to be Milla's over-the-top reaction to losing Harry and the baby. Ed supposed it was possible that her hormones were out of whack. She certainly wasn't thinking straight.

That would be his task today, he decided as he stood staring through a dusty window into the murky depths of the empty shop. He had to bring Milla to her senses, had to convince her to withdraw her application before she was committed to something she'd quickly regret.

Almost five years ago, he'd stood by and watched her marry Harry, knowing full well that it could only end in disaster. He wasn't going to let her walk into a second catastrophe.

He wondered what time she came down for breakfast, but the question had barely formed when he heard a sound coming from the back of the shop.

An intruder?

Frowning, he tested the shop's door, and it fell open at his touch. He stepped quietly inside.

'Hello?' he called. 'Is anybody there?'

When there was no answer, he moved forward stealthily. 'Can I help you?'

'Ed?'

Milla appeared in the doorway.

'Ah.' Feeling slightly foolish, he offered her a sheep-ish smile. 'Hi.'

Hands on hips, Milla frowned at him. 'What were you doing? Why are you sneaking around?'

'I thought there was an intruder in here.' He shrugged. 'And I was sure you were still asleep.'

Milla rolled her eyes. 'I've been up since before six.'

'But you weren't in the dining room for breakfast.'

'I had breakfast here.' She pointed to an electric jug beside the sink in the corner. 'A tub of yoghurt, a ba-nana and a mug of tea, and I'm set for the day.'

Ed gave a shrugging shake of his head.

'I hope you slept well,' she said after a bit.

'Like a baby.' He grimaced and a small silence fell while they both studied the bare concrete floor.

He guessed that Milla was as reluctant as he was to mention the obvious fact that she'd found him last night, sprawled on her bed, sound asleep and stark naked.

'Sorry I missed our dinner date—er—dinner dis-cussion,' he said, steering the conversation away from that particular danger zone. 'I hope the duck was good.'

'It was delicious, thanks.'

'And I hope you were—uh—comfortable last night.'

'I was perfectly comfortable, thanks. In your room,' she added, not quite meeting his gaze.

The air around them seemed to thicken and grow hot.

'Have you had breakfast?' Milla asked, after a bit.

'Sure.' He patted his middle. 'An inelegant suffi-ciency.'

'I'm sure you were starving.'

'Yeah.' But it was time to remember that he hadn't come here to discuss his appetite. Narrowing his gaze, he said, 'So why are you over here so early?'

'I thought you might want to sleep in, and I needed to make a start. I'm making an inventory of all the equipment that's here, and working out what I still need.'

'Jumping the gun, aren't you? You don't even know if the council will accept your application.'

She made an impatient sound of annoyance. 'I'm quite certain they will, Ed. They're very keen.'

Ed bit back a swear word. 'You're setting yourself up for failure, Milla. You can't do this. It's obvious this town is on its last legs.' He flung out an arm, indicating the empty shop and the equally empty street. 'Where are your customers? The last people who tried to run this place failed.'

'They didn't know enough about baking. Their bread wasn't popular.'

'Are you sure you can do better?'

'Absolutely.'

'Milla, if you really want to work, you could get a job in a top Sydney hotel. The sort of work you were doing before you married.'

'You want me back rubbing shoulders with the rich and famous?'

'Yeah? Why not?' When Ed first met her in London, she'd been a brilliant hostess for VIP guests.

Arms folded, shoulders back, jaw jutted, Milla eyed him with bolshie determination. 'I've had enough of that life, Ed. If I see another spoiled rock star I think I'll puke. I was born and raised in this town. We lived in Matheson Street, but I spent half my life in this shop. Before I started school, I was playing down here with pieces of dough, making my own bread rolls for my lunches.'

A fighting light burned in her lovely green eyes.

'All through high school, I sliced and packed bread each morning before I caught the bus to Parkes. Afternoons, I worked out the front on the counter. Saturdays, I helped my mum to make her famous fruit lattice pies.'

Ed was impressed, but he didn't let it show.

'After I finished school, I started learning the trade properly. I know baking inside out,' Milla said finally.

'And you couldn't wait to get away from it.'

She glared at him. 'I was young and impatient, with a head full of big dreams.'

He nodded his acceptance of this. He supposed she was remembering, as he was, where her youthful dreams had led her—overseas to a wide range of interesting and fulfilling jobs, but, eventually, into the arms of his dangerous young brother.

No point in rehashing that now.

He nudged the conversation back to where he wanted it. 'So, I guess you've written a business plan? You've prepared a break-even analysis and a profit and loss forecast?'

She sent him a drop-dead look.

'Do you know your fixed costs?' he continued. 'The profit you're likely to make from each sale?'

'Go home, Ed. I don't need you marching in here and throwing your weight around, spoiling everything.'

'I'm trying to save you from the misery of starting up a business that's doomed to fail.'

'That's very thoughtful of you.' She lifted her chin and eyed him steadily. 'But I'd prefer a little faith.'

It was then that he saw behind her bravado and glimpsed the vulnerable girl clinging to her last shreds of dignity and hope. And damn it, he felt a flicker of admiration. He quickly stifled it. A good businessman always trusted his head, not his heart.

'Tell me about the equipment,' he said, changing tack. 'What have you got and what do you still need?'

'Do you really care?'

'Give me a break, Milla. Of course I'm concerned.'

She pursed her lips, then seemed to relent. 'OK. I have a big oven that's been here since the nineteen fifties. It's great. No worries there. I have gas cookers, a big bread mixer and a refrigerator and freezer. I'll need more measurers and cutters and things like piping bags and nozzles, but they're not a huge cost. I could do with an orbital mixer, but that can wait.'

'An orbital mixer? What's that?'

'It's good for the smaller things—cakes, cream and icing.'

'I guess you need scales for weighing things?'

Her eyes widened with surprise. 'Yes, scales are very important. Dad used to have a really expensive set. I don't know what happened to them.'

'Where are your parents now? Will they be around to give you back-up support?'

'Heavens no.' A warm smile lit up her face. 'They're on a cruise. The Mediterranean this time. These days, they're always on cruises and good luck to them. They've worked hard and they've earned their chance to have fun.'

Her smile faded, replaced by a look of defiance. 'I need to do this, Ed.'

Deep down, he understood. Milla wanted to throw herself into hard, honest labour, as if it would somehow heal her past hurts.

'What if you fail?' He had to ask this. 'What if you

reject Harry's money and try this—this hare-brained scheme and end up with nothing?'

'That's not going to happen.'

'Milla, how can you be so sure?'

She simply smiled. 'Try all you like, Ed. You're not going to change my mind.'

CHAPTER FOUR

To Milla's relief, Ed's farewell was unsentimental. A handshake, a kiss on the cheek.

Unsmiling, he wished her good luck.

'Good luck to you, too,' she said, and he looked at her strangely. 'Good luck with explaining everything to Gerry.'

His mouth tilted in a wry smile. 'Thanks, I'm sure I'll need it.'

The smile disappeared as Ed got into his red hire car and the look in his eyes then made Milla's throat ache.

They both knew this was the last time they would see each other, but she hadn't expected Ed to look quite so bleak. And she certainly hadn't expected to feel bereft, pierced by a sadness that was quite different from how she'd felt when she'd lost Harry or her baby.

As Ed zoomed off down the long straight road she stood on the footpath, watching his red car grow smaller and smaller. When it finally disappeared, she let out her breath with a deliberate whoosh and she waited for the expected sense of relief to wash over her.

To her surprise it didn't happen.

Instead she felt strangely empty.

It was such an annoying, irrational response. Now

that Ed was gone, she was free. Free of the Cavanaughs, free to put her mistakes behind her and to make a success of the rest of her life.

As she went back inside the bakery it didn't make sense that she couldn't stop thinking about Ed. Bizarrely, her thoughts weren't centred on his warnings about her business. She was remembering, of all things, the first time she'd met him when she was working at The Hedgerow Hotel in London.

The job in Knightsbridge had been the pinnacle of her working career. She'd earned it, of course, having worked hard at all the usual jobs that backpackers grabbed when they left Australia. She'd been a barmaid in Kent and a baby-sitter-cum-cleaner in a French ski resort. She'd worked on organic farms in Italy for free meals and board, and eventually she'd ended up in London with a job on a reception desk in a hotel chain.

To her surprise, the position had really suited her. She hadn't minded working different shifts, and handling computers hadn't fazed her. She'd managed to be cheerful and diplomatic with difficult guests and queue jumpers, and she'd quickly picked up that it was worth taking time to deal with all the little things that counted.

As a result, Milla had been promoted quite quickly, and when the manager of the VIP luxury service for the hotel's executive clients retired, she was offered his position.

She'd loved this role and she'd thrown herself into it. She made sure that platters of fresh fruit were available on arrival for VIP guests, and whatever they wanted— even pink champagne in their bathtubs—was accommodated.

As well as arranging beauty spas and massages, it

had been her responsibility to make sure these special guests never had to wait for a dinner table, or theatre tickets, or a clean towel. She had even sent staff out to buy gluten-free bread at awkward hours.

Whether the VIP guests were charming or childish, aloof or overfriendly, Milla had taken their peccadilloes in her stride. Keeping them happy had been a daily challenge to which she'd risen conscientiously.

It was while she'd been working in this role that she'd met Ed. She would never forget the way he'd come striding into the hotel lobby just on nightfall, straight from a transatlantic flight. Tall, dark and dignified in a long black winter coat, he'd sent the hearts of female guests and staff fluttering.

Milla hadn't been immune to his impact. Not by any means. Until then, she'd never met any man who made her heart-rate quicken on first sight, but, despite his attractiveness, she'd made sure her manner was pleasant and friendly, and scrupulously professional.

Ed had come to London on business, of course, working very hard with late meetings and hasty dinners and Milla had facilitated several private, one-on-one hearings with European businessmen that had apparently been highly productive.

'You're an amazing asset here,' Ed had told her when he was leaving. 'I'll look forward to seeing you next time I'm in London.' He was dangerously handsome, especially when he looked into her eyes and smiled.

To Milla's dismay, she'd felt a warm blush that wouldn't go away. 'I'm actually moving on,' she'd told him. 'I think I'm a nomad at heart, and I've been in London for almost two years.'

He didn't try to hide his disappointment. 'Are you going back to Australia?'

'To America, actually. I've been offered a job in California.'

Such a gorgeous smile he'd given her then. 'Which hotel?'

'The Ritz-Carlton.'

'Fabulous. You never know.' Silver sparks had shone in his grey eyes. 'We might meet up again.'

Looking back, Milla could see the way her life had taken a crucial turn that day. She and Ed *had* met up again, of course. He'd made sure of it.

And who knew how things might have turned out if she'd been a little braver?

Ed was troubled as he burned up the miles down the highway. He knew he could never persuade Milla to give up her bakery plan. His efforts to do so had been a total waste of energy. She would almost certainly fail, but no one was going to talk her out of this.

As his hands clenched the steering wheel and his chest tightened he warned himself to let this go. It was Milla's problem, not his. He'd done his duty and she was an intelligent woman with the right to make her own decisions. Her own mistakes.

Again.

Thing was—despite his concerns, he couldn't suppress a niggling admiration. Having spent almost his entire adult life behind a desk or in boardrooms, he could totally understand the appeal of breaking free of the mould.

Heaven knew there'd been days when he'd wished he could throw off the shackles of shareholder expectation and escape the office to climb a mountain or canoe the Amazon, or sail around Cape Horn.

But Milla running a bakery?

No way. That made no sense.

Ed was still a little shell-shocked after seeing her with her hair covered by a scarf as she tackled cobwebs and wielded a mop and bucket. So different from the woman who'd always been so carefully groomed and dressed in up-to-the-minute fashion. So different from the first time he'd seen her working in the London hotel.

That day she'd been wearing a simple but chic black dress, a perfect foil for her pale skin and flame-coloured hair. He remembered her poise and the glint of elegant jewellery as she'd walked towards him with a warm smile.

She'd extended her hand. 'Hello, Mr Cavanaugh. Welcome to The Hedgerow.'

Ed had enjoyed his share of classy women, but there'd been something about Milla Brady that had woken a response beyond the ordinary. He'd been as fascinated by her efficiency as he had by the sheen of her hair, and her beautiful smile.

One evening during his stay, while he'd waited in the private lounge for an important meeting with a business contact from Brussels, he'd invited Milla to keep him company.

With a little encouragement, she'd told him about the places she'd visited in Europe, the sights she'd seen and the people she'd met. Her conversation had been so easy and entertaining that she might have been a high-class hooker.

She wasn't, of course. Ed's discreet inquiries had ruled that out. She was just damn good at her job. But she epitomised, he'd realised, his idea of the perfect woman.

Then she'd told him she was moving to America, and, although he didn't believe in astrology, he was quite sure his stars had been perfectly aligned. The fact that he lived in New York and Milla was going to California was a minor problem. With a brother in LA, Ed could use his out-of-town status as the perfect excuse to invite a woman he hardly knew to a party.

Harry's thirtieth birthday party had been timely. And it had been, of course, a lavish Beverly Hills affair. No expense spared. An orchestra, massive urns with towering flower arrangements, waiters in white coats and bow ties, guests from Hollywood's A-list.

Amidst the expensive gowns, the mirrors, the marble and chandeliers, Milla, in backless cream silk that showed off her moon-pale skin and bright hair, had looked completely at home in the glamorous crowd. And to Ed she'd looked utterly enchanting.

The night had gone well until he'd kissed her.

Even now, he could never look back on that party without a painful stab of self-reproach. He'd always thought of himself as urbane and cool, but he'd handled that night like a ham-fisted youth.

The evening had unravelled when he'd gone to fetch Milla another drink. While he was away, a gaggle of girls from Harry's set had gathered around her.

Returning, drink in hand, Ed had heard their conversation through a small forest of potted palms.

'What do you think of American guys?' one girl had asked Milla.

'I'm reserving judgement,' she'd told them smoothly

and then she'd laughed. 'But I must say, I wasn't in London this long before a fellow kissed me.'

'Those British guys are quick off the mark,' suggested another girl.

'Or American guys are damn slow on the uptake,' joined in another.

Laughter had rippled around the group, and Ed waited for it to die down before he joined them and handed Milla her mai tai cocktail. Even so, there'd been a momentary lull when he arrived, and in the quietness Milla's eloquent gaze had met his.

She must have known that he'd overheard their conversation and its implied challenge, but she hadn't seemed in any way embarrassed, and it had made every kind of sense to Ed to find the first opportunity to lure her out into the moonlit garden.

The grounds of Harry's mansion were perfect for strolling—smooth lawns and winding paths and shadowy pockets of palms or fragrant shrubbery.

'It's so lovely and warm here,' Milla had said as they walked past a lily pond where silver moonlight streamed. 'It reminds me of Australia.'

'Do you miss home?' he asked her.

'Sometimes. Not often. It's ages since I've been back. Luckily, my parents have retired, so they can visit me over here.'

'And how have you found America so far?'

Milla smiled, and her green eyes sparkled knowingly in the moonlight. 'I like my job. America's fun,' she'd said. 'Everyone's so friendly.'

'But the men are slow off the mark.'

She stopped walking. Her silk dress shimmered whitely and her skin looked wonderfully soft. 'It was just silly girl talk, Ed. I was playing along with their game.'

'But it's true, isn't it?' He took her hands in his, holding her cool fingers lightly. 'You haven't been kissed by an American?'

Her eyes became luminous. 'No, I haven't,' she admitted softly.

'That's a crime,' he said.

Her response was a breathless laugh.

'In fact,' he said next, 'I'm quite sure it's a crime in at least seven states.'

His heart was drumming as he settled his hands on her slim waist, which was crazy given that he'd kissed hundreds of girls in the moonlight. But, alone with Milla Brady, he had difficulty keeping his voice steady. 'It's most definitely a crime in California.'

As he leaned in she swayed towards him and their lips met in an easy and friendly hello. Warm and pleasurable and sweet. But within moments, everything changed. Ed had been lost. Lost in her yielding sweetness, lost in her eager response and the warm press of her slim body to his.

He kissed her hard and long and it felt like destiny, as if he'd been waiting all his life for this woman. This night. This moonlight. When he kissed her breasts through the thin silk of her gown, she went a little wild and he was quite sure she would have run away with him then, if he'd asked her, or even if he hadn't asked and had simply taken.

Perhaps she brought out the gallant knight in him, or perhaps he'd been a little afraid of the strength of his own passion... After all, the Cavanaughs were ladies' men, but they never lost their hearts.

On the brink of tipping into madness, Ed broke the kiss, but Milla remained entangled in his arms, her chest heaving against his chest, her head on his shoulder as their ragged breathing slowed.

'I'm not sure *that* kiss was legal,' he said eventually, trying to lighten the intensity of what had passed between them.

Her response was so soft he hadn't caught it, but she was no longer smiling. In fact, she looked worried. Very worried indeed.

After her passionate response, this didn't quite make sense. Ed couldn't think what to say. He'd been quite sure she hadn't wanted to discuss what had just happened, and he certainly hadn't. Small talk seemed somehow impossible, so he'd led her back, walking in silence via a wisteria-scented path, to the safety of the party.

Harry was standing near the door as they came inside. Golden haired, smiling, devilishly handsome, he was holding a champagne bottle. 'I wondered where you'd got to, Ed.'

Harry called to a waiter for two more glasses. 'You two look like you need a drink.' As he poured bubbles into Milla's glass his charismatic smile brimmed with sympathy. 'Beware of my big brother.' He managed to sound both sincere and amused. 'Ed spends too much time stuck in boardrooms and he doesn't really know how to party. He can be a bit of a wet blanket.'

'I'm having a perfectly lovely time,' Milla assured him.

'Are you?' Harry's gaze was shrewd as he studied her and then he'd looked at Ed. 'Hmm,' he said, slipping his arm possessively through Milla's.

Ed felt a prickle of apprehension. *No,* he'd thought. *No. Harry won't. He can't possibly.*

But of course, Harry could and he did.

He gave Milla his most charming smile. 'I should warn you, my dear, Ed peaks early and the night is young.'

She laughed, pulling gently away.

Harry's grip on her arm tightened. 'Besides, it's my birthday, and I demand your charming company for the next half-hour.'

As Milla surrendered and was borne away, she looked back over her shoulder to Ed, shooting him a look of amused bewilderment. 'See you later,' she mouthed.

Watching her leave, laughing at something Harry whispered in her ear, Ed felt powerless. It was Harry's party and there were too many guests to make a scene.

Besides, having witnessed his parents' fights so often during his early years, Ed abhorred family scenes.

His grandmother had sensed this back when he was seven. 'You're going to be our family's anchor, Ed,' she'd said.

It was a vocation he'd taken to heart, but there'd been many times since that he'd regretted his restraint on that fateful evening. He'd known from the start, and with chilling certainty, that Harry had had no qualms about stealing the girl his brother had invited.

And thirty minutes was all it had taken.

CHAPTER FIVE

PAINT ROLLER IN hand, Milla was poised on a trestle balanced between two ladders when the phone rang. Fortunately, the phone was in her jeans pocket, and she didn't have to scramble down to answer it.

'Milla? Or should I say Michelangelo?' Heidi chirruped. 'How's the painting?'

Milla laughed. 'Believe it or not, I'm actually enjoying myself.' She beamed at the snowy ceiling above her and at the two walls already covered with lovely, fresh paint, the rich hue of thick cream. 'And I'm almost halfway there.'

'Well done.' After a beat, Heidi added, 'But it's a pity the handsome American didn't hang around to help you.'

Milla's heart gave a twist, much to her annoyance. 'Who told you about Ed?'

'A little bird whispered.'

'A bird by the name of Sherry, I suppose.'

'Well, yeah, you know this town's always desperate for a bit of juicy gossip. Sherry was raving on about this American of yours. She said he looked like—'

'He's not mine,' Milla cut in.

'But he looks like a film star, right?'

Milla sighed. She'd been working hard to erase Ed from her thoughts. 'He's Harry's brother, Heidi. He was here on—on family business.' Although Milla had shared the awful news about Harry's death with Heidi, she'd skipped details of exactly how that news had been delivered. 'Now he's well and truly gone. Back in the States.'

'Oh.' Heidi sounded disappointed, but she quickly switched to her usual cheerfulness. 'Anyway...getting back to the subject of painting...do you need a hand? I could come tomorrow. Mum's offered to look after the kids.'

'Gosh, that's very kind of you, but I hope to be done by then. With luck, I'll finish this first coat before lunch today and get the second coat on this afternoon.'

'Wow, you've set a cracking pace. You always were one for a challenge, Mills.'

'I suspect the painting will be the easy part of this particular challenge. I'm sure I'm going to need help closer to opening day. That's when I'll start to panic.'

'I'll warn Mum in advance and make sure we're free.'

'Thanks, you're a doll. That would be brilliant.' After the out-of-whack values in Harry's set, where her friends were constantly trying to compete, it was so refreshing to have a friend who genuinely wanted to help. 'Heidi, I don't suppose you know anything about writing a business plan?'

'Sorry, haven't a clue. Do you really need one?'

'The Bellaroo Council's asking for it. Apparently, it's a requirement for their dirt-cheap rental agreement. I'm afraid I bluffed my way through that bit and told them I'd have a plan within the week.'

'Hmm. I don't suppose they're offering to help you write the plan?'

'Unfortunately, no,' Milla said.

'Well, I could ask Brad. He's done a few business courses.'

'Thanks. That could be helpful. I'd probably only need a few pointers.'

'Why don't you come out to our place tomorrow evening? Kill two birds with one stone. You can talk about business schemes with Brad and we can have a barbecue. It'll be fun. You can celebrate finishing your painting.'

'Thanks. I'd love to.'

'See you around six-thirty?'

'Perfect. I'll bring a fruit pie. I've been practising with Mum's old recipe.'

Heidi laughed. 'Fab. I'll be generous and supply the ice cream.'

Milla was grinning as she pocketed her phone and turned back to work. She was incredibly grateful for the way Heidi had picked up their friendship exactly where they'd left off, as if the intervening years hadn't made a jot of difference.

Now, making her way carefully along the trestle plank to the radio she'd balanced on top of the ladder, she flicked a knob, and found a country and western station. Music filled the shop, one of the happier songs about a rollicking cowboy, and she sang along with it as she ran the roller through the tray of rich creamy paint.

As she spread it in smooth swathes on the wall she realised that she'd told Heidi the truth. She found this painting job unexpectedly satisfying. The worst part had been the preparation and cleaning the dingy old walls with sugar soap, but now it was so rewarding to see the way a fresh coat of paint could revitalise the space.

Once the walls were finished, she planned to scrub the terracotta floor tiles till they shone, and *voilà*! The bakery would look fresh and welcoming again.

Throw in the added fragrance of freshly baked bread and—

'Milla!'

A masculine voice boomed from below.

Milla turned and when she saw who it was she almost slipped.

It couldn't be. It was impossible. Where had he sprung from?

'Hey, don't fall.'

Two strong hands gripped her calves, just below the knees.

Ed. Why on earth was he here? He was supposed to be safely in New York by now.

'You startled me,' she accused shakily. 'You shouldn't creep up on a girl like that.'

'I tried knocking, but you had that music so loud you couldn't hear me.'

Milla was still too shaken to defend herself. 'You can let me go. I'm quite steady, now,' she lied.

Grim-faced, Ed released her, and Milla was at her most dignified as she set the roller back in the paint tray and carefully lowered her butt to the trestle. From this point she could normally get to the floor quite easily, but today Ed was there to lend a helping hand.

The fact that she was still trembling was his fault, of course.

'Mind if I turn the radio down?' he asked.

'Be my guest. Turn it off.'

The music stopped and the sudden silence seemed to fill the shop. But now that Milla had both feet on the ground, she demanded answers. 'What's happened? Why aren't you in America?'

'No drama.' Ed looked annoyingly calm as he stood there, hands resting lightly on his hips as he let his gaze linger on her beautiful walls. 'You're doing a good job,' he admitted grudgingly.

She couldn't help saying, 'I'm happy enough with the way it's going.' But it was annoying to be pleased by his comment when she should have been interrogating him.

Now that she was beginning to recover from her shock it was time to ask questions. 'Get to the point, Ed. You still haven't told me why you've come back. What's the problem?'

There had to be a problem. Why else would he come back all this way?

Ed's throat worked and he shifted his gaze to the street, as if he'd been suddenly gripped by an almost boyish nervousness. 'I—er—stayed to look after a spot of business in Sydney, and I happened to run across a few things.'

Huh? 'What kind of few things?'

Frowning, he squared his shoulders, as if he was de-liberately throwing off his initial shyness and returning to his default mode as Mr Serious. 'I found some of the equipment you need.'

At first, Milla couldn't imagine what he meant. 'Equipment for the bakery?'

Ed shrugged. 'You haven't already ordered them, have you?'

Stunned into silence, she shook her head. 'I wanted

to get the place cleaned up first. I was planning to start researching on the Internet this weekend.'

His brow cleared and a slow smile lightened his eyes. 'Well, I found one or two items that might be useful. So I'll bring them in now, OK?'

'I—I guess,' she said faintly. 'Can I help you?'

'No, no. I'm fine.'

There was a ute parked in the street outside, she realised now, and the tray back held several large cardboard cartons. Heavy cartons, judging by the bulging muscles in Ed's arms as he carried them into the shop.

'Will I take them through to the back?' he asked.

'Thanks.' Milla decided that he must have been working out. Or he'd started buying T-shirts a size too small. Either way, the display of masculine strength was almost as distracting as her curiosity about the boxes he carried.

Her eyes popped when she read the first label. 'An orbital mixer?'

'I hope it's the right size.'

'Wow, Ed.' She found a knife and began to cut the packaging tape, whipping the cardboard flaps open. 'It's perfect. So new and shiny.' She'd been planning to investigate second-hand equipment. It was mind-boggling to think that Ed had remembered her passing comment.

She was stunned and grateful...but just a tad worried. Why had he done this? Could it be a new strategy for regaining Cavanaugh control?

But it was hard to suppress her excitement when the next box revealed a top-of-the-range set of bakery scales.

'They're beautiful.' Milla touched a fingertip to the

rim of the shiny steel bowl. 'They're brilliant. Thanks so much.'

The scales were followed by more boxes holding all manner of lovely things—dough dividers, pie cutters, a tiered rack of bun pans.

Milla was quite dazed. 'I can't quite believe this.'

'I happened to come across a warehouse with all this stuff and it seemed crazy to walk past.'

'Which warehouse?'

Ed looked away and mumbled the name of a Sydney suburb, and, despite Milla's excitement and gratitude, she was sure she smelled a rat.

'So you just happened to be walking down a Sydney street and, blow me down, if there wasn't a bakery warehouse right in front of you? I suppose the mixer and scales were on display in the window?'

'Look,' Ed said, jutting his jaw defensively. 'I have no plans to interfere with your new venture, Milla. I know you don't want our money. You made that very clear.'

'So you'll let me pay you for these things?'

A dark stain coloured his neck. 'That's not necessary.'

Milla sighed. 'So what's this about, then? Come on, Ed, spill. Are you going to tell me you're concerned about the demise of Bellaroo Creek?' Sarcasm crept into her voice. She couldn't help it. 'You're doing this for the good of the town?'

He met her acerbic challenge without blinking. 'My grandparents used to live in a small country town like this.'

It was the last answer Milla had expected and she felt caught out. Winded.

She simply couldn't imagine the wealthy, lavish-living Cavanaughs coming from humble roots in a small rural town. The picture wouldn't gel.

Then again, why would Ed make up a story like that?

Warily, she offered him a puzzled smile. 'Well... if that's really what's driving you... On behalf of the Bellaroo Creek Residents' Association, thank you very much, Mr Cavanaugh.'

'You're welcome.' Slowly, Ed returned her smile and their gazes linked and held, and ridiculous tingles zipped and zapped through Milla.

Then Ed nodded through the doorway to the half-painted shop. 'But I've interrupted your work. The paint on your roller will dry out.'

'Yes. I'd better get back to it.'

'I don't suppose you have a second roller?'

Milla's jaw dropped so hard it hurt. How many surprises was this man planning to spring on her? She did have a second roller, but surely Ed didn't really plan to help?

'I'm not going to turn straight around and drive back to Sydney,' he said. 'I don't fancy another five hours on the road today, so I have an afternoon to fill in. I may as well make myself useful.'

Once again, Milla hesitated, torn between her desire to remain stubbornly independent and her gratitude for his apparently good-hearted generosity. And somewhere above and beyond these hovered an extra problem, the problem she'd always had with Ed Cavanaugh. The strong, almost frightening attraction she felt in his presence, and the scary certainty that a relationship with him would take her well out of her depth.

Five years ago, this fear had sent her running into

the supposedly safer arms of his lighter-hearted, fun-loving brother.

And what a mistake that had been.

Now, Milla didn't want to feel attracted to any man, certainly not to Ed. She was making a fresh start as far away as possible from her past mistakes.

Just the same, she knew she shouldn't be in such a stew over one afternoon in Ed's company. This evening he would stay at the pub and tomorrow morning he would be gone again, finally and for ever. Where was the harm in that?

Feeling calmer now that she had this sorted, she reached into the box of gear she'd bought from the hardware store in Parkes. 'It's kind of you to offer to help.' She broke open the plastic packaging and handed him a brand-new fluffy roller and tray. 'Ever used either of these before?'

'Of course.'

She couldn't hold back a cynical smile. 'Honestly?'

'Well…not in the last twenty years.'

It truly was like stepping back in time.

Ed hadn't spent an afternoon like this since he was fifteen when he'd helped his grandfather to paint their barn. Back then it had been fall in Michigan and Ed could still remember the scent of apples in his grandparents' orchard and the gentle lilt in his grandfather's voice as he delivered his homespun philosophies while they worked.

Today, Ed couldn't believe how good it felt to be away from boardrooms and meetings and phone calls and the constant crises and pressure of his Cavanaugh Enterprises. It was such an agreeable change to be working at a task that demanded a totally different kind of concentration.

In no time he was crouching low, taking desperate pains to paint as close as possible to the skirting in a neat straight line. It was unexpectedly rewarding to take as much care with the smoothness of his paint-work as he normally took over calculating a new investment strategy.

When Milla stopped for lunch, they perched on stools at the stainless-steel table at the back of the shop. Milla made thick, tasty cheese and salad sandwiches, which they washed down with mugs of hot tea, and while they ate she explained that she'd moved into the rooms above the shop, and that this area would double as her kitchen.

They chatted about the best positions for the new equipment, and Milla explained the steps involved in producing dozens of bread loaves. She certainly seemed to know the process well, Ed was relieved to note, and although he itched to fire a host of questions to test her business knowledge he held his tongue.

Just as they were finishing their meal, a fat ginger cat stalked regally into the room, his ginger tail waving above him like a flag.

Milla's face was alight as she squatted to scratch the cat's neck. 'Blue, you beautiful boy, how are you this afternoon? Have you had a good morning?'

'Why would you call an orange cat Blue?'

Her eyes sparkled. 'It's an Aussie thing. Goes way back. I guess it shows how contrary we are. We often call redheads Blue or Bluey.'

Ed smiled. 'Were you called Blue at school?'

'Sometimes.'

'So where does this Blue live?'

'Here. He's mine.' Her laugh was light and silky. 'At least, he seems to have made this place his home. He just wandered in one day and stayed.'

'So you've already taken in a stray?'

Her chin lifted. 'Yes, Ed, I have. You got a problem with that?'

He gave a non-committal shrug and Milla returned her attention to the cat, her face soft and loving as she spoke of sweet nothings with him. Watching her more intently than was wise, Ed decided that this was, almost certainly, how she would have looked when she talked and played with her baby.

The baby she'd lost.

Thinking about it now, he felt his throat constrict and he had to look away. She'd hardly mentioned the miscarriage, but it was patently clear that this plan of hers to return to her roots was her way of dealing with her loss.

He was still absorbed by these thoughts when Milla asked, 'What about you, Ed? Are you a cat or a dog person?'

Neither, he almost said, but out of nowhere he remembered carefree summers in Michigan when he and Harry had roamed and fished along the Kalamazoo River. Their grandparents' golden Labradors had been their constant companions and the dogs' loping, loyal faithfulness had added an undeniable dimension to the boys' adventure.

'I guess I'd go for a dog if I had a choice.'

'I like dogs, too, but once the bakery's up and running, I won't have time to exercise one.'

Ed thought about the long hours of hard work ahead of her and grimaced. Had she really thought this through? She couldn't simply dabble at baking, then give it up if she got tired of it. Did she really know what she was letting herself in for?

He might have asked, but he hadn't come here to start another argument. By the same token, he didn't want to think too hard about why he *had* come back to Bellaroo Creek.

When Milla had challenged him, he'd thrown up his grandparents' hometown as a convenient excuse, but he hadn't really been thinking about them when he tracked down the bakery warehouse in Sydney, had he?

His focus had been his concern for Milla taking on this huge task on her own. That, plus his guilty awareness that the Cavanaugh family had let her down badly.

His family owed her.

He said, 'At least Blue will help to keep the mice population down.'

Milla flashed a grateful smile. 'Exactly. And I've decided that every bakery needs a cat.'

Her smile was as fond as a lover's as her gaze followed the tom when he stalked off once more, heading to the back door where a food bowl waited on a sunny step.

The damn cat had no idea how lucky he was.

They got back to painting and the afternoon seemed to fly. It was almost dark by the time they finished. Milla turned on the light switch to admire their handiwork.

'I love it,' she said, gazing with deep satisfaction at the smooth cream surfaces. She could already imagine these beautiful walls lined with racks of freshly baked loaves of smooth golden bread. She would have wicker baskets, too, with an assortment of bread rolls, and she would place pottery urns in the shop's corner, filled with sheafs of dried wheat. It was going to be gorgeous.

She sent Ed a triumphant grin. 'Thanks for your help.'

'I think we've done a great job. It was fun.'

He looked as if he meant it, which worried Milla. She was used to seeing Ed looking buttoned-down and serious in an expensive Italian business suit, busy with his BlackBerry. Today he looked too different, so relaxed, in his dark grey T-shirt and jeans. And way too attractive.

And now she noticed a scattering of fine, cream-toned spots sprinkled through his raven-dark hair. And there were larger splotches on his cheek and shirt. 'Yikes, you've got paint all over you.'

In answer, his gaze rested on her chest and a slow smile warmed his handsome face. 'I see we're two of a kind. Your sweater looks like a Jackson Pollock painting.'

It couldn't be that bad.

But it was pretty bad, Milla had to admit, when she looked down at her paint-splattered front. 'I guess I'm still getting the hang of this painting gig.'

She shrugged. 'And you need to get cleaned up and hop over to the pub. You're welcome to use the sink. There's a towel and soap and at least the paint is water based.'

She might have offered to wash out his T-shirt, but the thought of Ed standing around shirtless brought on a vision of him lying naked on her bed and she was assaulted by a fresh flurry of zaps and tingles.

'I suppose I'll have to hunt for Sherry again,' Ed said as he went to the sink and began to scrub paint spots from his arms. Milla took one look at his muscular forearms and hurried out the back to clean the rollers at an outdoor tap.

When she came back inside, Ed was still at the sink, now with his shirt off, washing his hair. Just as she'd feared, the sight of his powerful shoulders and strong, muscular back was enough to give a healthy woman problems with her breathing.

Ed reached for a towel and dried his face and hair. Then he looked up and grinned at her.

Help. Had he caught her ogling him?

'I'll book a table for dinner,' he said. 'You'll join me, won't you?'

Milla was quite sure that a dinner date couldn't be wise. This was supposed to be her post-Cavanaugh life.

Ed's smile was several versions of engaging, however. 'I promise I won't fall asleep on you this time.'

'If we're to have dinner together, it should be my shout,' Milla said stiffly. 'I'd like to thank you for the equipment and for your help today and…everything.'

He shook his head. 'I need to make up for last time.'

It would be silly to fight over this, but it would help if she understood exactly why Ed was here and why he was being so helpful and friendly. She'd assumed he was trying to keep some kind of control over her, but why would he need to do that now that both Harry and his baby were…gone?

She supposed Ed might be genuinely concerned about her, which was kind, even noble. But she would find his kindness so much easier to accept if she could forget about that long-ago kiss…

Then again, it was plain crazy and unhelpful to think about that kiss now. Ed had probably forgotten it years ago. At this moment, he was calmly waiting for her answer.

'Thank you,' she said as lightly as she could manage. 'I'd love to join you for dinner. Let's hope the duck and mushrooms are still on the menu.'

As soon as Ed was gone, Milla hurried upstairs to the three rooms above the shop that were now her living quarters. In the days when her parents had owned the bakery, they'd only used these rooms for storage and they'd lived in a large and comfortable house two streets away.

Now, however, Milla quite liked the idea of living above her shop. Her needs were simple—a bedroom, a tiny sitting room and bathroom were sufficient. The only furniture she'd bought during her one trip to Parkes were a bed and an armchair, but in time she would paint these rooms in rich, warm tones, and she would shop for a sofa, a bookcase and a rug and other small items to make the space homely.

She had plans for the skinny strip of weedy yard at the back of the building too. She wanted to create a small courtyard, a chicken coop, a veggie patch...

As she pulled her sweater over her head her muscles complained. Her arms were tired from all the painting. A hot shower would help and—

Heavy footsteps sounded on the tiled floor in the shop below. Milla froze. Surely that couldn't be Ed back already?

Hauling her sweater on again, she went to the top of the stairs. 'Who's there?'

'Just me,' came Ed's voice.

It was annoying to feel suddenly anxious. 'What's

wrong?' she called as she hurried down. 'Can't you find Sherry?'

'I had no problem finding her,' Ed said. 'But the pub's fully booked.'

'You're joking.' Milla gripped the post at the bottom of the stairs as she stared at him in disbelief. 'But that's ridiculous. I stayed at the pub for over a week and I was the only guest in the place for most of the time.'

'Apparently there's a rodeo on this weekend.'

'Oh.' Milla winced. 'Yes, that's true.' But it had never occurred to her that the pub might be full. And now it was too late for Ed to set off back to Sydney.

She pictured him spending the night here with her, and a riffle of disquiet that was close to panic made her shiver. 'I should have thought of that—I'm so sorry, Ed—I should have warned you.'

He didn't look worried, however. 'Most of the guests are staying out at the rodeo till late, so I still managed to book a table for us for dinner.'

'But where will you *sleep*?' Her voice made an embarrassing squeak on the final word.

Ed looked mildly amused. 'I'll be fine. Sherry tells me there are rooms in motels in Parkes and that's only an hour away.'

'Oh…yes, of course.' Why hadn't she thought of Parkes, instead of uselessly panicking? 'I'm sorry I can't offer you a spare bed. There's only an old camp stretcher here, and you wouldn't want that.' Ed was used to nothing less than five-star hotels. 'I slept on it for the first couple of nights over here, and it's not very comfortable.'

Ed merely shrugged at this and looked mildly amused. 'If I took the stretcher, I wouldn't have to drive to Parkes. We could enjoy a bottle of wine with our dinner.'

Milla was quite sure she could do without the wine.

But Ed was in persuasive mode. 'You must agree we've both earned a relaxing meal and a glass or two, and I'd rather not drive and risk an encounter with your police.'

What could she say without sounding inhospitable?

'Let me see this stretcher,' he said.

The stretcher would do, Ed decided, although exactly why he was willing to sleep on it was a question he wasn't keen to examine.

Chances were, he'd look back on this interlude in Bellaroo Creek as temporary insanity. But if he was pushed to give an answer, it wouldn't be too hard to justify this return visit. He felt responsible for Milla. After all, he'd introduced her to Harry, and as a result her life had veered way off course. And everyone knew he was a responsible kind of guy.

His desire to hang around here had nothing to do with any finer feelings for the woman. Ed knew better than that. Sure, his blood leapt whenever he saw Milla, but falling for a person who couldn't love you back happened to nearly everyone. He'd learned to accept this particular wound. It was permanent but bearable. A war injury he'd collected on the Cavanaugh family battleground.

Some time back, Ed had decided that relationships weren't for him. They weren't straightforward like running a business. There were no secure, blue-chip investments. Relationships were all about risk and loss, and it was easier to remain an emotional bankrupt.

Discreet affairs were fine. Anything deeper was out of his league.

As for now…his mission was simply to support Milla's goals, to do everything within his means to ensure her success and future happiness.

With that achieved, he could leave Australia with a clear conscience, and he would finally close the door on this less than happy chapter in his life.

And now that Milla seemed to have accepted his plan to stay, she'd changed from looking scared to being resigned and practical.

'If you're going to stay here, I'll fetch the sleeping bag from upstairs,' she said. 'It belongs to a friend and it's designed for sleeping in the snow, apparently, so it should keep you plenty warm enough. And you'll need to use my bathroom, so go bring your things in, Ed, and I'll get a towel for you.'

She shot him a cautious glance. 'The bathroom's upstairs.'

'I'll wait till you've finished using it.'

'All right.'

The sleeping bag was duly unrolled and Ed prowled around the downstairs area until the sounds from the shower stopped and Milla called down, 'All yours…'

When he ascended, she was already in her bedroom with her door firmly shut. But the tiny bathroom was filled with her flowery scent, and he was all too conscious that she'd been in there, bathing.

He shut off his damned imagination before it got him into all kinds of trouble.

CHAPTER SIX

MILLA CAME DOWNSTAIRS in black leggings and elegant ankle boots teamed with a bright, leaf-green knitted top that fell to mid-thigh. It was a simple outfit but with her bronzed-copper hair and pale skin, she looked sensational.

Ed swallowed. 'You look wonderful.' *Like an elven princess.*

To his dismay, she blushed and looked embarrassed. 'Let's go,' she said quickly. 'I'm starving.'

Outside, a blustery wind whipped at them as they ran across the road. The pub's carpeted foyer was warm and welcoming, however, and Milla was tidying her hair, tucking bright curls behind her ear, when her phone rang.

'That's Heidi's ringtone,' she muttered, digging her phone out of her shoulder bag. 'Excuse me, Ed, I'd better answer it.'

'Of course.'

She'd already explained about her friends Heidi and Brad, and he waited while she went to the doorway, where she stood with her back to him, looking out at the street while she talked.

Ed tried not to listen, but he couldn't help pricking up his ears towards the end of her conversation.

'No, that's perfectly OK, Brad,' she said. 'I totally understand. Your farming and marketing plans would be very different from a small retail outlet like mine. Yes, yes, that's good advice. I'll find an accountant. Or a good business advisory firm. Got it. Thanks for letting me know. No worries. Yes, tell Heidi I'll ring her in the morning about the barbecue. Thanks again. Bye.'

As she turned off her phone and slipped it back into her bag, she gave Ed a self-conscious smile. 'Sorry about that, although I guess you're used to taking endless phone calls in public.'

'Endless,' he agreed. 'But over the weekend, I've switched off my phone and I've had my calls diverted to my long-suffering PA. I'm loving the silence.'

'So no withdrawal symptoms?'

'Not even the occasional twitch.'

Milla smiled and they were both still smiling as they went down a silky oak-panelled passage to the dining room where they were greeted by a very wide-eyed Sherry.

'Nice to see you again.' The girl beamed at Ed and shot Milla a look brimming with significance as she showed them to a table near the fire. Their table was set for two with a white linen cloth and starched napkins, shining silver and a small crystal vase of yellow jonquils.

'This is rather elegant,' Ed remarked with genuine appreciation as Sherry went off to fetch their selected wine.

'Bellaroo Creek springs yet another surprise.' Milla looked around at the other diners sitting at equally attractive tables. 'Perhaps the hotel staff lifted their act for the busy weekend.' A small smile played. 'Most rodeo visitors don't need starched tablecloths, but it shows the staff can achieve wonders when they try.'

'As we have discovered today,' said Ed.

She nodded and her smile grew broader. 'The shop's going to look fabulous, isn't it? I can't wait to get the bakery up and running.'

Ed hated to burst her bubble by pointing out that a few painted walls were a long way from a successful business. And he couldn't pretend that he wasn't concerned by her end of her phone conversation.

I'll find an accountant, she'd said. *Or a good business advisory firm.*

It was pretty clear she was seeking business advice, which her friend, Brad, had been unable to provide.

There was no way she'd ask for his help, Ed accepted grimly, but, although this rankled, he wouldn't let it spoil the night.

After the wine arrived, had been tasted and poured, he raised his glass. 'Here's to the Bellaroo Bakery.'

'And to all who sail in her,' Milla responded with a laugh.

It was the first time since he'd arrived in Australia that she'd looked so happy and relaxed. And so beautiful with the firelight reflected in her smiling green eyes.

I'm mad, he thought. *I should get out of here now.*

He paid attention to the menu instead, and they both ordered a Chinese wonton soup to be followed by the famous duck and mushrooms. And while they waited for the food, they drank their wine and talked about their favourite meals and their childhood pets and the similarities and differences between America and Australia.

Over the soup, they tossed around the pros and cons of baking organic bread made from specialised wheat.

When the duck arrived, their conversation was reduced to 'Yum' and 'Mmm' and blissful smiles.

'This is really good,' Ed said, spearing a dark plump mushroom with his fork.

Milla grinned. 'Not bad for the back of beyond.'

'Not bad for anywhere.'

'I hope the chef stays.'

'He might if the "Save Our Town" scheme works.'

'Yes.' Milla's bright smile faded and was replaced by a thoughtful frown. 'I hope it doesn't turn out to be a pipe dream.'

Unable to help himself, Ed asked, 'Is everything OK? With your business? I—I couldn't help overhearing part of your phone conversation.'

The shutters came down on Milla's face. 'Everything's perfectly fine,' she said. 'It—it's nothing I can't handle.' She paid studious attention to the food on her plate.

It was damn frustrating to know that she might have a problem he could easily solve. 'Milla, if it's to do with the business, you know I can almost certainly help you.'

'You've already done enough.' She set her fork on her plate and sat back, lifting her napkin to dab at her lips. 'I don't need your help. Anyway, you have to go back to New York, and I'll be fine. There are any number of people here who can help me.'

'So you admit you do need help?'

Milla sighed. 'Has anyone ever told you, you're like a terrier with a bone?'

'All the time.'

She smiled again then. And Ed smiled back at her.

They seemed to be doing rather a lot of smiling this evening. Her eyes were the clearest green and breathtakingly beautiful, and he sensed a moment of connection that made his head spin.

Eventually, he said, 'So now you know that I'm not going to give up, why don't you just tell me your problem?'

'It's not really a problem.' She looked around at the other diners who were scattered about the room, intent on their own conversations, and not paying them the slightest attention. With a resigned lift of her shoulders, she said, 'It's just that I need to write a business plan. It's part of the council's lease agreement.'

'Hang on. You mean to say, you've moved into the bakery, you've started painting the walls, I'm buying equipment, and you still don't have a proper agreement?'

Milla narrowed her eyes at him. 'This is the bush, Ed. The council trust me. They know I'll get it done.'

'Have you ever written a business plan?'

'You know I haven't, but I'll engage someone who knows how to write one.'

'Like me,' he said quietly. 'I know these things inside out and backwards.'

'You're leaving in the morning.'

'I don't have to.'

It wasn't strictly true. There would be all hell to pay if he stayed away much longer, but Ed had lived his whole life being the conscientious Cavanaugh. Perhaps he could blame being down under for this sudden, reckless reassessment of responsibilities.

'I don't know,' Milla said with a worried shake of her head. 'There's a world of difference between the business dealings of Cavanaugh Enterprises and anything I'm trying to do here.'

'Business is business.' Ed topped up their wine glasses. 'It's simply a matter of scale.'

She seemed to consider this as she watched him cautiously over the rim of her glass. 'So what would you cover in my business plan?'

'Well…for a start, you'd need to show your estimated costs of production, your expected capacity and cash flows, and your break-even point. I guess the council would be interested in the range of your potential market, your sources for materials. The degree to which your business will help the locals. And you'd—'

'OK. OK.' Milla gave a smiling eye-roll as she held up her hands. 'I think you've made your point, Ed. You could write my business plan in your sleep.'

Sherry arrived to take their plates. 'Can I tempt you guys to try our desserts?'

'Just peppermint tea for me,' said Milla.

Sherry pulled a face. 'I'm not sure we do herbals. I'll have to check. What about you, sir?' She batted her eyelashes at Ed. 'Can I tempt you to strawberry pavlova?'

'I'm happy with the wine,' said Ed, impatiently returning to his conversation with Milla even before the girl had left. 'Given half a chance, I could pull a business plan together for you in a day.'

'Do you know enough about this district?'

He shrugged. 'I can jump on the Internet to find any info I need. There'll be government websites with demographics for the region.'

Milla's peppermint tea arrived. 'I found a tea bag,' Sherry said, but she was too busy tonight to linger, which was probably a good thing, given Bellaroo

Creek's hunger for gossip. After she'd left them, Milla took a thoughtful sip of her tea and then set her cup on its saucer with excruciating care.

Her face was super serious as she looked at him. 'Why are you doing this, Ed?'

It was a good question. A damn good question. Milla was probably worried that he had designs on her. But he wasn't a fool. He'd learned his lesson when she rejected him on their very first date.

They'd shared one kiss, a kiss of earth-shattering passion—he'd never experienced anything close to the powerful magic of it before or since. And while she was sitting chastely opposite him now, she'd been wild and uninhibited on that night. A sexy, heart-stopping miracle. He had known then that he'd found someone very special.

And yet...

Ed considered the abysmal way Harry had treated her. And he thought about the angry phone call he'd received from his father two days ago. Gerry had berated Ed, as if he were somehow responsible for the loss of his grandchild...

And Ed knew Milla had every right to ask why he, another Cavanaugh, was here uninvited, offering to hang around and help.

He gave her the simple truth. 'I believe my family owes you.'

His family owed her...

Ed's answer sideswiped Milla. Her teacup rattled against the saucer as she set it down again.

She'd been so sure Ed was here to maintain some kind of Cavanaugh control over her. She'd been certain that his selfish, egocentric family assumed that *she* owed them a debt, simply because they'd allowed her into their hallowed, wealthy midst.

And now, at the mere mention of his family, the memories she'd been trying so hard to bury flooded her thoughts. The long lonely nights, Harry's drunkenness and gambling. His endless affairs.

Her husband had hurt her and let her down in so many ways, and his hard, self-centred mother had always taken her son's side and never supported Milla.

As for Gerry Cavanaugh, Harry's father—he'd practically ignored Milla until he'd learned that she was pregnant with his grandchild, and then he'd sent Ed and a damn PI after her.

Now here was Ed, the one member of the Cavanaugh family who had every right to resent her, claiming instead that they owed her.

'I don't understand,' she said. 'Are you talking about money? My inheritance?'

Ed gave her a long, hard look without speaking. Eventually, she felt flustered and dropped her gaze. What was he implying? That the family should have warned her about Harry? Protected her?

But she'd been a grown woman, free to choose, to make her own mistakes.

And Ed's presence in Bellaroo Creek was a constant reminder of those mistakes. 'I crossed hemispheres to put it all behind me,' she said.

Ed let out a heavy sigh. 'I get that. And to be honest, I don't blame you.'

Across the table, he sent her another sad smile, a smile that made her heart beat faster and raised more questions. Questions she dared not ask.

Milla was relieved that the meal had come to an end. There'd been times when it had felt dangerously like a date, and she was glad to hurry back through the cold winter's night to the bakery.

Again they took turns using the bathroom, a situation Milla found ridiculously intimate, so she was tense as a trip wire when it was time to say goodnight.

'I'm afraid I only have one small heater,' she confessed.

'In your bedroom?' Ed asked.

'Well…um…yes…'

Amusement glittered in his eyes and she feared he might tease her about this, but then he seemed to think better of it. 'I'll be toasty in my thermal sleeping bag.'

'OK, I'm impressed,' announced Heidi as she stood at her kitchen window, supposedly tossing a salad, but mostly staring out into her backyard where Brad and Ed were manhandling steaks on the barbecue. 'I mean, I'm *seriously* impressed.'

'With my cherry pie?' asked Milla sweetly.

Heidi made a scoffing sound. 'I'm sure the pie's delicious, but, man, your *American* is hot!'

'You sound like Sherry,' Milla protested. 'And you should know better. You know he's not *my* American. He's Harry's brother and he's here on business.'

'But whose business?' Heidi asked darkly. 'That's the big question.'

This silenced Milla. She was beginning to wish she'd come up with an excuse to back out of this evening. Instead she'd weakened and phoned Heidi, who had of course insisted that she bring Ed to the barbecue.

'I've sliced the baguette,' Milla said now in an un-

subtle bid to change the subject. 'Would you like it but-
tered?'

'That'd be great,' Heidi muttered impatiently. 'But
I'd rather you answered my question.'

Milla sighed as she reached for the butter dish. 'Ed
came here to settle family business.'

'But he stayed here to help you with *your* business?'

'He's a control freak. He can't help interfering.'

'Nice try, Milla.'

'Excuse me?'

'I'm sure a man like Ed Cavanaugh only interferes
when and where it suits him,' Heidi remarked archly.

Milla fumed for a moment. 'Ed thinks his family
owes me. He's always had a well-developed sense of
responsibility.'

'And that's not the only thing that's well developed.'

Milla wisely ignored this. 'Ed also knows business
plans inside out and backwards.' It felt weird to be quoting Ed almost word for word, but with Heidi backing
her into a corner she was at a loss. And quoting Ed was
certainly safer than discussing his physical attributes.
After another day of working in his close proximity, answering his endless but surprisingly patient questions
about her plans for the bakery, Milla was all too familiar with the way Ed looked and behaved.

All day, while she'd painted window frames, Ed had
worked on her business plan, and his presence had dom-
inated her awareness. Mostly, she'd been trying to digest
the astonishing reality that a top-flight business mag-
nate from New York was paying such earnest attention
to her little country bakery's profit and loss potential.

While they'd talked about the range of goods she
might sell, about staff she might need to employ...

While they tossed around ideas like leaving samples of her baked goods in the general store during the lead-up to opening day... Milla had also been stealing glimpses in Ed's direction simply because the breadth of his shoulders was so impressive.

Much to her embarrassment, she'd found herself also admiring the sheen of his dark hair and the neat line it made across the back of his neck as he hunkered over her laptop.

It was mere aesthetic appreciation, of course. Nothing personal. But unfortunately, Ed had caught her peeking. More than once. He'd looked up, their gazes had met, and she'd seen a flash in his eyes that had sent flames shooting under her skin.

She'd tried to cover up with the lamest of excuses, making a comment that she'd never seen him wearing his reading glasses. She was quite sure he'd seen right through her.

But despite these slips, she wasn't *interested* in Ed. Not in *that* way.

'Admit it, Mills,' Heidi persisted with a grin. 'The starry guys have always fallen for you. Remember high school? And Heath Dixon?'

'I'd rather not.' A flash of unpleasant panic scorched Milla, followed by an involuntary shudder.

Heidi seemed oblivious to her reaction. 'You had the sexiest guy in the whole school practically begging you to go out with him.'

'Aren't you being disloyal to Brad by suggesting that some other guy at school was the sexiest?'

'Brad doesn't have a jealous bone in his body.' Heidi's face softened, transformed from plain to exceptionally pretty as her cheeks were warmed by an affectionate smile. 'Brad knows how I feel about him.'

Milla watched as Heidi sent a dreamy, private smile out of the window and she felt a sharp pang of envy.

So, I guess that's what true love looks like.

'But Heath Dixon was something else,' Heidi continued emphatically. 'He was hot-looking and dangerous…and drooling over you, Milla. And every girl in Year Twelve was pea green with envy. You never explained why you went on one date with the guy and gave him the flick. We were stunned and in awe at your heartlessness.'

If only they knew…

Milla had never told anyone, not even Heidi, about what had happened on that one night with the loathsome school heartthrob. 'Heath Dixon was a creep,' she said now, bitterly.

Heidi stared at her with wide-eyed interest. 'Do tell.'

'Actually, no. I'd rather drop the subject of men. I'm afraid it bores me to tears. I'm completely over the male of our species. I'm here to resurrect a bakery.'

'Milla, you can't turn your back on men altogether. Apart from any other considerations, they make up half the world's population.'

Milla shrugged. 'I'm over falling *in love* with them, that's for sure. And I'm certainly over the Cavanaughs. After a disastrous relationship with one member of that family, I have zero interest in getting involved with another.'

'Well, yes, I can see that's fair enough.' Heidi nodded sagely, but it wasn't long before she was smiling again. 'But you have to admit…it was so cute when you arrived here tonight and Ed was so desperately keen for us to admire your cherry lattice pie. He looked so proud...and so *fond*...of you.'

'That's because I remind him of his grandmother.' Heidi hooted.

'No, it's true. He bought me these pastry cutters, you see, and—'

'*Ed* bought pastry cutters?'

'Yes. I told you he was a control freak. He had to make sure I had decent equipment.'

'Sure, sure,' Heidi's voice purred with sarcasm.

'Apparently, his grandmother used to let him cut the pastry strips when he was a kid,' Milla explained.

Heidi's eyebrows hiked. 'Well, there you go.'

Watching her friend's amused disbelief, Milla conceded that the picture of Ed helping her with pastry strips was totally incongruous with his normal persona as Mr Big of the business world.

It had been fun today, teaching him about pastry and explaining how she would plan things when she had to make a dozen pies at one time.

Heidi had said… *He looked so proud…and so fond… of you.*

The word *fond* lingered in Milla's mind, like a favourite passage of soul music.

'Anyway, I'm very glad you brought Ed out to our place,' Heidi continued chattily. Once again, she cocked her head towards the view through the window. 'Brad's certainly enjoying his company. The two of them seem to be getting on like a house on fire.'

Curious, Milla stepped closer to the window, and she saw Ed with Brad, looking extremely relaxed, drinking beer and chatting and laughing as they kept a weather eye on the sizzling food. Her heart gave a strange little lurch.

Having so recently and vocally avowed that she was *off* men, she felt like a hypocrite. This sentimental pang was a mistake, a momentary aberration.

Perhaps she could blame the perfect setting. Heidi and Brad seemed to have a knack for making their home look welcoming and heart-warming, like something you'd want to photograph. Not the perfect shots of magazines though, but appealing and lived-in and somehow just right.

They'd built their own barbecue and set it in a pretty paved courtyard, and tonight there was a wood fire burning brightly, and the air was filled with the mingled smells of smoke and frying onions. Heidi had strung glowing Chinese lanterns between the trees, and she'd covered the outdoor table with a red gingham cloth and fat yellow candles.

Despite the cold winter's night, a backyard had never looked more inviting. And Ed had never looked more relaxed, Milla thought. He almost looked as if he belonged here.

'Watching from here,' said Heidi, standing close to Milla's elbow. 'A person could be forgiven for thinking that those two were old, old friends.'

It was true. Ed's and Brad's backgrounds were worlds apart, but they were probably around the same age, and they were both tall and broad shouldered and athletic and they seemed to be talking and laughing non-stop.

'It's pretty amazing, actually,' said Milla. 'Ed's usually frowning and earnest.'

Just then Brad said something that was greeted by

a crack of laughter from Ed. She wondered what they were talking about.

'So, I'm assuming Ed's keen on your bakery idea?' Heidi prompted as she lifted a potato salad from the fridge.

'I'm pretty sure he thinks I'm mad. But he does seem intrigued by the Save Our Town scheme.'

'Well, Brad's totally committed to *that.* Keeping the town alive depends on keeping the school open, and now that Thomas has started in Year One, Brad's on the Parents and Friends'. Poor Ed's probably copping an earful right now.'

Milla smiled. 'If he is, he doesn't seem to mind.'

'True.' Heidi surveyed her prepared salads with a critical eye. 'OK, these are good to go. Let's get them outside and join the party. Can you bring the bread and the pepper and salt? I'll drag the kids away from their DVD.'

She lifted her voice. 'Thomas! Lucy! Dinner's ready.'

'I want to sit next to the man,' insisted a small, golden-haired cherub as she looked up at Ed with huge brown eyes.

'How about asking nicely, Luce?' her mother re-minded her. 'And the man's name is Ed.'

'I want to sit next to *him*,' the little girl said with pointed emphasis.

Heidi groaned. 'Did I hear the word *please*?'

The golden angel smiled impishly at Ed. 'Please, Man.'

'Lucky me,' he said gallantly, but he was wondering what he was in for as he shifted over and made a space beside him on the long wooden stool. 'Shall I lift you up?'

'No, I'm a big girl. I can get up all by myself.' With a certain amount of huffing and puffing, the small person scrambled onto the seat. Once she was in place, she pushed a golden mop of curls out of her eyes and beamed at Ed with a grin of unholy triumph. 'See, I'm up.'

'You are indeed.' He couldn't help smiling. He'd never before been at such close quarters with a diminutive female, and he was intrigued.

'I'm going to have a sausage wrapped in bread with tomato sauce,' she announced importantly.

'And salad,' warned Heidi.

Her daughter's small pink lower lip drooped. 'I don't like salad.'

'No salad, no sausage.' Heidi followed up her stern warning by serving a spoonful of lettuce with cherry tomatoes and cucumber and carrot onto her daughter's plate.

Ed watched, mildly amused, half expecting a wail of protest. Instead, he found two large brown thickly lashed eyes gazing up at him solemnly. 'Do you like salad, Man?'

'I love salad,' he assured her.

Next moment, as her mother turned her attention to her brother, the little girl scrambled to her feet. Standing on the seat, she leaned into Ed with her mouth pressed against his ear. 'I'll let you have my salad,' she whispered in great excitement, as if she were bestowing an enormous honour. 'Don't tell Mummy.'

In a flash, she was down again, sitting demurely as

her father set the desired, crisp and crunchy sausage on her plate. 'You want sauce, pumpkin?'

'Yes, please, Daddy.'

Ed swallowed an urge to chuckle. He'd never realised that feminine wiles started so young. He was enjoying himself immensely, and out of nowhere snuck the most surprising thought. What would it be like to have a small cherubic imp of his own?

He'd hardly given fatherhood a thought, but this evening was having a strange effect on him. From the moment he'd arrived at Heidi and Brad's farmhouse, he'd felt as if he'd stepped back in time. Not that Milla's friends were out of touch with the modern world. They were fully informed and up-to-date, but there was a beguiling, old-fashioned and slower-paced atmosphere about their home and family that took Ed straight back to gatherings at his grandparents' farm in Michigan.

Truth be told, Thanksgiving in Michigan when he was around fifteen was probably the last time Ed had eaten a meal where the adults and the younger generation sat down together. The adults, of course, had been his grandparents, not his parents.

Ed couldn't remember ever sharing a meal with his parents. He could barely remember his mother and father dining together. They were divorced before he'd turned five. After that, whenever he'd stayed in his father's new house, his dad had rarely been home at mealtimes. He'd always been at board meetings, or business dinners or benefit breakfasts.

As for Ed's mother, she'd always slept in late in the mornings, never rising before he had to leave for school, and her evening meals had usually been liquid and consumed on the couch in front of the television. If she'd been awake to say goodnight to Ed, she'd reeked of whisky and slurred her words. He'd been brought up by a succession of nannies and maids.

Sitting here now, pretending not to notice as pieces of tomato and cucumber were surreptitiously deposited onto the side of his plate, Ed watched Milla's smiling eyes and listened to her laughter mingled with that of the others, and he felt unexpectedly, deeply...happy...

And at home.

It was a shock to remember that, no matter how comfortable or welcome he felt here, he was still an outsider. Cavanaugh Enterprises existed in another dimension. It might as well have been an alien planet where the inhabitants had calculators instead of hearts.

Tonight, Ed couldn't help thinking how different everything had been on the one night he'd taken Milla to a social gathering. Harry's glittering, over-the-top birthday party in Beverly Hills had been light years away from this simple, unpretentious backyard barbecue.

Of course, Ed could see now why Milla had been so easily dazzled...

He could also understand why she'd come running back home when the scales had finally fallen from her eyes.

CHAPTER SEVEN

ED DROVE BACK into town along quiet country roads, past starlit paddocks where owls sat on fence posts, waiting to pounce on unwary field mice, or whatever strange equivalent they had in Australia. He drove past dark clumps of gumtrees and over rattling, narrow, one-lane bridges. And in the view through the windshield, a shining full moon bobbed through drifts of gauzy white cloud.

He couldn't remember the last time he'd had such a clear view of a moonlit landscape and sky. The scenery was almost mystical and it seemed to cap off a perfect evening. He felt uplifted. Touched by magic.

Beside him, Milla sat in silence, her bright hair and delicate profile limned by silver light as she stared out at the countryside, apparently lost in thought.

'I really enjoyed tonight,' he said when the silence had gone on a little too long. 'Thanks for letting me tag along.'

'I'm glad you enjoyed it.' Her voice was friendly enough, but she quickly lapsed back into her musings, huddled inside her padded jacket. It wasn't long before she folded her arms, hugging them to her chest. A fencing-off gesture, if ever Ed had seen one.

But he was in too good a mood to let her body language deter him. 'I enjoyed meeting your friends,' he said. 'Brad's a cool guy. Great sense of humour.'

Milla roused. 'Brad's always seen the funny side of life. I suspect that's why Heidi fell in love with him.'

'No doubt.' Momentarily, Ed's happy mood was sideswiped by memories of his brother's laughter and charm. Almost certainly, Milla had been attracted by Harry's broad grin and his love of telling a clever joke, a skill Ed had never mastered.

With an effort, he shook off disturbing memories. 'Brad has a really good head on his shoulders. I'd say he's a very good farmer.'

'Seems to be.'

'I had a good chat to him about growing organic wheat.'

'Really?' Milla sounded incredulous. 'Why?'

Ed shrugged. 'We were talking about your bakery and how there's a growing market for organic products.'

'Oh.' Now she sounded prickly. 'Brad never said anything about it to me.'

'We talked about a ton of stuff,' Ed reminded her. 'But if you did decide you wanted to try organic wheat, Brad would be a good guy to talk to.'

Milla nodded, apparently satisfied. 'Heidi says Brad's very passionate about saving Bellaroo Creek's school.' Unfolding her arms, she sat straighter. 'Isn't it great that they're encouraging those young families to come here by offering farmhouses for a dollar a week?'

'Yeah, maybe. I'm still not sure it will work.'

She turned to him. 'Do you have a better idea?'

Ed couldn't resist the obvious challenge. 'What Bellaroo Creek needs is a proper injection of capital.'

'*Whose* capital?'

'Anyone's. I'm talking in theory, right?'

'I suppose your family could buy the whole town if you wanted to.'

He gave a non-committal shrug as he changed gears and eased the ute around a sharpish corner. 'The thing is, if the place looked more prosperous and was offering solid employment, people would come and pay full rent.'

'Hmm...' Milla sounded doubtful. 'Nice theory. I suppose you might get faster results. But apart from the fact that no one's likely to risk their money on this out-of-the-way place, if one person or a company owned all the businesses in a town, whose town would it be? How would you develop a sense of community?'

'I don't see why—'

'And how could you guarantee that the people you employed would have children to keep the school going?'

'Simple. You'd screen them during the interview process.'

Milla appeared to consider this. 'OK, tell me this, Ed.' She paused as they reached the main road and Ed waited for a truck to pass before turning. Once they were whizzing down the bitumen, she said, 'Do you think the people who came here to work for you would have the same sense of self-worth as someone like me, starting from scratch, doing the hard yards and the renovations by myself?'

'Ouch.' He shot her a sideways glance and caught the almost warrior-like challenge in her eyes. 'That came from the heart.'

'Country towns need heart.'

'And dollars.'

Almost as soon as he'd said this Ed knew it was a mistake. He wasn't even sure he totally believed his own argument. Before Milla could pounce on him, he hurried to cover his tracks. 'Don't get me wrong. I'm not arguing with you. You made a good point. Self-worth is important. In the long run, I'm sure it's more important than fiscal worth.'

'Wow,' Milla said softly. 'Coming from a Cavanaugh, that's a very interesting statement.'

Yeah... Ed had surprised himself, trotting out that little homily. Maybe he'd been down under too long and he was starting to view the world upside down.

But there was no hiding from the bleak truth. Milla was right about his family. The Cavanaughs epitomised the old cliché. Money hadn't bought them happiness. Ed only had to think about his father, obstinately courting his fourth bride-to-be, while knowing that his chances of success were on a par with his previous marriages...

His mother was even sadder. Lonely, bitter and sharp tongued, she had certainly found no comfort in her wealth.

It was hard to tell with his young brother, Charlie, but he was young, so there was still hope.

As for devil-may-care Harry...

Or me?

Ed sighed, while beside him Milla seemed to shrink back into her silent deliberations. Once again she was huddled with her arms folded tightly, her face turned away as she stared out through her side window.

They reached the outskirts of town, slipping past the small white weatherboard church and the endangered little school with its playground and football field, past the straggle of houses that rimmed the main street. Soon, Ed brought the ute to a stop outside the darkened bakery and as the motor died he heard Milla let out a heavy sigh.

All evening at the Murrays' place, she'd seemed to be light-hearted and happy. The return of this low mood bothered him. 'You OK?'

Milla started and frowned at him. 'Sorry?'

'I asked if you're OK. Is something bothering you?'

She shook her head. 'I—I was just remembering… something…'

Whatever she was remembering, it troubled her. One of the few streetlights in the town was shining in on them, illuminating her lovely face, and her anxiety was clear to Ed. He could see its shadows in her eyes and in the sad twist of her mouth.

He was trying to think of the right thing to say when she pushed her door open and hopped out, fishing in her bag for her keys. He climbed out, too, locked the ute and joined her as she opened the door.

The smell of fresh paint greeted them as they went through the shop, carefully skirting the piles of drop sheets on their way to the doorway at the back. The ginger cat came forward with a soft meow and rubbed his sleek body against Milla's legs. Milla gave him a scratch, then turned on the light, bringing the bakery's workroom to life with its thick brick walls and stainless-steel benches and the back section filled by the massive rotating oven.

Ed saw his stretcher in the corner, complete with neatly rolled sleeping bag, and he felt his spirits sink. The stretcher wasn't too uncomfortable, but he knew he wasn't ready for sleep. He hoped Milla wasn't planning to scurry upstairs straight away.

'Is it OK if I make coffee?' he asked.

She looked surprised. 'Are you sure you want coffee at this time of night?'

'I nearly always have coffee at this time of night.'

'Oh? OK.' With a strangely distant smile, she hurried to the fridge and extracted a packet of ground coffee. 'This do?'

'That's fine, thanks. I'm happy to make it. Care to join me?'

She hesitated, and the shadow of whatever was bothering her seemed to hover above her. Ed stamped on an urge to pull her in his arms, to kiss her soft, brooding mouth. But the urge was persistent. He longed to kiss her smooth white throat, kiss any and every part of her till she was purring with happiness and pleasure.

Instead he sent her an encouraging smile, a trick that had worked in the past with almost any woman.

Her answering smile was a shade wistful. 'I won't have coffee,' she said. 'It'll keep me awake, but I could do a peppermint tea.'

'Perfect.'

While Milla collected a tea bag from the pantry cupboard, Ed set the kettle to boil and measured coffee into the pot. As he slipped bright mugs from hooks, she opened the buttons on her jacket and shrugged out of it, letting it drop onto a spare stool before she dragged another stool for herself. Then she slumped forward with her elbows on the bench, her chin in her hands.

Her Renaissance gold hair glowed warmly beneath the harsh fluorescent tube and her face was a picture of mournful self-absorption.

Ed knew it was stating the obvious, but he had to ask. 'That bad memory still bugging you?'

He half expected her to remain sunk in gloomy silence, or to tell him it was none of his business. He was surprised when she lifted her head.

'It's pretty stupid,' she said. 'Just something Heidi mentioned tonight. Something from our high-school days.'

'High school. *Sheesh.*'

Milla's green eyes widened. 'Didn't you like school?'

'It was OK. I guess it's the same for everyone. Some good memories, some I'd rather forget.'

She nodded soberly. 'I wish I could forget this one.'

Ed felt a clutch in his heart. He'd never thought of himself as chivalrous, but tonight he longed to come to her aid, to at least make her smile again. But his gallant thoughts were pierced by the kettle coming to the boil and he made a business of filling her tea mug and the coffee pot.

'Do you want to leave the tea bag in?' Such a safe, practical question.

'For the moment, thanks.'

Then he asked, carefully, 'So you haven't talked to Heidi about this…problem?'

Milla shook her head. 'She doesn't know a thing. No one does. Except—except the person concerned. I—I've never told anyone else.'

Was that wise?

Ed wasn't sure what to say. Unless he was discussing investments or business, his counselling skills were nix. 'I've never been one for baring my soul,' he admitted. 'But they do say that talking about stuff is supposed to help.'

To his surprise, a small smile shone in Milla's eyes. 'Are you offering to be my Father Confessor, Ed?'

The very thought made him nervous as hell. He swallowed to relieve the broken-glass sharpness in his throat. 'Sure. If it would help. It would go no further. I can promise you that. I mean, it's not as if I'll be hanging around after this weekend.'

Milla's hands were shaking as Ed handed her the mug of tea. She was actually feeling sick now. Sick with tension. And fear.

She'd been fine earlier this evening when Heidi had let fly with her chance comment about Heath Dixon. At the time, Heidi had merely stirred a bad memory that Milla had quickly dismissed. Once she'd been absorbed into the give-and-take of lively chatter around the barbecue she'd more or less forgotten about it.

Later, though, when she and Ed were driving home, the memory had stolen back into her thoughts. This time, alone with Ed and the dark night, the memory had turned vicious, rousing a chain reaction of panicky thoughts about dates and boyfriends. Harry and Ed.

Successive memories had spilled, one after the other, stirring her anxiety and guilt till she thought she might burst.

And now...

Why on earth had she thrown that half-smart Father Confessor question at Ed?

Poor man...

Being the conscientious and responsible type, he was now waiting...expecting...

She watched his strong, squarish hands as he lowered the plunger, carefully, slowly, like a true coffee lover.

He had no idea he was actually a part of her problem. How could she tell him?

But perhaps a more pressing question was…how could she pass up this chance to explain the things she'd wanted to explain years ago? In another day Ed would be gone back to America, and this time he would certainly stay there. This was her best and last chance to set the record straight.

But man, she was nervous… And where should she start?

She stared at a spot on the floor, trying to summon her scattering courage. Closing her eyes, she said quickly, 'When I was sixteen, a guy almost raped me.'

It sounded terrible to hear it out loud in the silent, almost echoing space. But perhaps it was like loosening a cork out of a bottle and the rest would come more easily now.

'A guy in high school?' Ed prompted gently.

Milla nodded. 'Everyone looked up to him as the school heartthrob. I was supposed to be incredibly grateful that he did me the huge honour of asking me out.' Nervously, she fiddled with the string attached to her herbal tea bag. 'But on our first date, when I wouldn't play it his way, he turned nasty.'

'You poor girl.'

It was helpful, the soft way Ed said this, as if he really cared. It gave Milla the courage to push on.

'I panicked of course, which made the guy madder, and then he got even more violent.'

She didn't look at Ed, but she heard the *clink* when he set down his mug and out of the corner of her eye she saw his fist clench.

'Does the son of a bitch still live around here?'

'He's long gone, Ed. Don't worry. That was one of the first things I checked when I came back.'

Ed nodded grimly. 'But you've never told anyone about this?'

'I couldn't face the gossip. It's the major downside of living in a small town. And as I said, this fellow was the school heartthrob. All the kids from here travelled to Parkes on the school bus. The other girls were jealous that he was paying attention to me. They knew as soon as he asked me out—he'd spread the word, I found out later. Everyone was waiting to hear what happened on our date.'

'I can imagine,' Ed said quietly.

'If they knew what really happened, it would have been hell. I just couldn't bear seeing the pity or curiosity in everyone's eyes. It was easier to let him tell his mates that I was frigid and he dumped me. I told my friends he was boring.'

Ed was frowning still, watching her with a thoughtful gaze. 'I presume he hurt you?'

Milla nodded. 'It was worse than I let on. I made an excuse that I'd tripped down the stairs. I should have won an Oscar for my brilliant acting. Even my parents believed my story about the bruises. No one ever dreamed the truth.'

Ed made a soft sound, a sigh or a groan—Milla couldn't be sure. 'I assume you told Harry,' he said after a bit.

'No. This was something from my old life and I was trying to reinvent myself after I left here. Besides, it would have been too heavy for Harry. He hated anything deep and meaningful.'

Ed scowled, but he didn't look shocked. 'I'm so sorry

for what happened, Milla. I wish there was something I could say or do to make the memories go away.'

What she needed was a hug—a comforting, platonic, Father Confessor–type hug. But she didn't deserve any further kindness from this man, not after the way she'd so hastily and rudely ditched him in favour of his brother.

What an idiot she'd been.

'Thanks, but I'm OK,' she said.

'I'm not so sure about that,' Ed said gently, and with that he came closer and gathered her in.

And after only a moment's surprised hesitation, Milla sank against him, absorbing the strength of his arms around her as she leaned into the comforting solidity of his chest and buried her face in the lovely softness of his expensive cashmere sweater.

What simple bliss a hug could be! Ed made her feel warm and safe. Comforted. There'd been precious little comfort for Milla lately, especially when she'd most needed it—after she'd lost her baby. In Ed's arms, she felt as if she'd been on a long, exhausting and dangerous journey, and had finally stumbled into a safe haven.

Resting her head on his shoulder, she couldn't remember when she'd felt so thankful.

Careless, selfish Harry had rarely tried to offer her comfort. She wasn't sure he'd known how.

Then again, she hadn't expected Ed to show this degree of thoughtfulness either. And when it came to surprises—the very fact that she could let Ed hug her without getting nervous was another revelation. The calmness she felt in his arms tonight was very different from that first night they'd gone out, when the intoxicating fire and passion of their kiss had frightened her.

But in the very midst of consoling herself with this comforting notion, Milla realised that her hormones had scooted way ahead of her thoughts. Already, she could feel her body reacting. Heat flared along her arms, and in her breasts, her stomach, wherever her body touched Ed's. Coils of longing tightened low inside her.

Perhaps it was just as well that Ed released her. But…oh, how she missed the power and warmth of him. Missed everything, actually, including—no, especially—the stirring excitement.

But she couldn't tell how Ed felt as he moved away to the safety of the far side of the workbench. He kept his gaze averted, although she could see that his mouth was a tight, downward-curving line.

'Thanks for the hug.'

He shrugged. 'My…pleasure.'

An awkward silence fell then, as if neither of them knew what to say. Almost simultaneously, they picked up their mugs.

'I hope your coffee's not too cold,' Milla offered.

Ed took a deep sip. 'It's fine.'

She removed her tea bag, squeezed the excess liquid, and dropped it into the sink. It was so quiet in the bakery she could hear the cat, back in his bed, purring in his sleep.

'So,' Ed said at last, with just the tiniest hint of a smile returning. 'Are *they* right?'

Milla shot him a look of confusion. 'Excuse me? They?'

His eyes glinted with brief amusement. 'They who say confession is good for the soul.'

'Oh.' She let out her breath on a soft sigh. Of course.

She'd told her story and Ed had hugged her better, so he thought her confession was complete.

Unfortunately, the hard part, the important part that concerned him, was still to come.

'Actually, Ed—' Her mouth was so dry now that her tongue wouldn't work, but she couldn't wimp out. She'd wanted to explain about this for so long. 'Actually, I'm afraid there's something else I need to tell you.'

It wasn't surprising that his eyes took on a new, wary alertness.

'It's something that still bothers me...something I feel guilty about.'

Ed frowned. 'There—there weren't repercussions? He didn't make you pregnant?'

'No, no, nothing like that happened. It's just that—'

She looked down at the remains of her peppermint tea, as if somehow the pale dregs could give her strength. Even though she was clutching the mug in both hands, she was shaking. She set the mug down. 'You see...ever since what happened in high school, I've had a sort of phobia. I've—I've always got panicky when I'm out on a first date.'

Her eyes filled with tears, and she blinked hard, desperate to be rid of them. She couldn't afford tears now. This was difficult enough for Ed, without making it worse by weeping. Men hated to see women cry.

Right now, Ed was standing as stiffly as a sentry guard on duty, and his eyes looked agonised. 'And you're telling me this because—'

When he stopped, Milla nodded. 'Because I panicked on our first date, when you took me to Harry's party. That kiss we had was so—' A suffocating heaviness pressed on her chest. Her eyes stung. 'It was so overwhelming,' she managed at last. 'I—I loved it, but it frightened me.'

Ed gave a stunned shake of his head, but in a matter of moments he was beside her again.

'Milla.' Her name was a mere whisper of breath.

'I'm so sorry.' She felt a little braver now that he was close. 'I've always wanted to explain. To apologise. I'm scared of things getting too passionate, you see? Getting out of control with someone I don't really know. I wanted to tell you, but it sounded so childish. I wanted to be sophisticated, like everyone else, but—' She sighed. 'I felt so silly.'

'Don't.' Ed's voice was strangled as he took her hands and clasped them in his.

As his warmth enclosed her she stopped shaking.

'Don't keep punishing yourself,' he said.

'But I've always felt bad about the way I behaved that night. Leaving you and going off with Harry. It was so immature. Stupid.'

'First-date syndrome,' Ed said softly.

She looked up sharply. Was he teasing her?

But no. Although he was looking at her with a strangely lopsided smile, there was no sign of teasing in his clear grey eyes.

'It's a well-documented phenomenon,' she said, joining his attempt to lighten the moment. 'And I believe I'm a perfect case study.'

But now, Ed's smile was dying. 'Thanks for telling me this, Milla. It actually means—' His throat worked as he swallowed. 'It means a lot, more than you probably realise.'

For an electrifying moment, as their gazes held, she saw a look in his eyes that almost stopped her heart. If she'd been braver, she would have followed the urgings that clamoured deep within her. She would have taken a step closer and kissed him.

Instead, she merely wondered.

What would it be like to try for one more kiss with this devastatingly attractive man? The mere thought sent excited shivers dancing over her skin. She could already imagine the first touch of their lips, gentle and testing. Then…as happy warmth spread through her there would be a little more pressure…and she would open her lips so she could taste him.

The thought made her dizzy with delicious antici- pation.

If only she were brave enough to try.

But now Ed's smile took an ironic tilt as he released her hands. Stepped back. And her lips, her whole body, went into mourning for what might have been.

'So…this begs the question,' he said, still holding that faintly sardonic smile. 'How did my little brother get it right? How did Harry handle your first date?'

'That's the thing,' Milla said with a resigned shake of her head. 'Harry didn't take me on a first date—not just the two of us alone—not for some time, at any rate. At first, there was always a crowd. Parties, sailing trips, night clubs. By the time we got…*closer*…we were more or less friends, and it…didn't feel like a first date.'

A corner of Ed's mouth quirked in a sad, wry little smile. Milla felt sad, too. Sad for the paths their lives had taken, sad because it was too late to do anything about it.

She was almost tempted to tell Ed her one last se- cret—that Harry had never roused her passions. Not really…

She supposed that was one of the many reasons their marriage had failed. But nothing could be gained by telling Ed about that now.

She watched him go to the sink and rinse out his coffee mug, watched his hands, watched his profile, and the way his shoulders looked so powerful, even performing this simplest action. She watched the way his dark hair fell forward onto his forehead. And a burning ache filled her throat. A terrible sense of loss swept through her, a chilling wave of misery.

It was far too late to realise that she loved him, that she'd fallen for him from the start, from that very first evening he'd swept into The Hedgerow Hotel on a wet London night, wearing his long black coat and looking so dark and dashing.

There was certainly no point in mentioning any of that, and there was only one sensible thing to do now that she'd confessed and more or less received Ed's absolution.

Despite the turbulence of her emotions this evening, she was still basically a prudent woman, so she did the sensible thing.

She said goodnight, and she went upstairs, while Ed got ready for another night on the stretcher.

CHAPTER EIGHT

ED WAS ALREADY awake when dawn crept into the bakery, spreading the first pale glimmers of wintry light. It wasn't so surprising given that he'd been restless for hours, tossing and turning on the narrow stretcher.

What a night.

When he'd first tried to get to sleep, he'd been bouncing from stunned disbelief over Milla's revelations to angry despair that he'd so easily let her slip away. It was patently clear to him now that he'd missed his best, possibly his only chance of true happiness.

Over and over, he'd kept remembering the way she'd looked as she'd told her story—so pale and vulnerable, and yet brave, too, determined to finally throw off the dark shadows of her past.

But as his mind went back to their first date—their one and only date—he asked himself why he hadn't sensed her nervousness at the time. Why hadn't he been more sensitive? Why hadn't he taken things more slowly?

The problem was, of course, that he'd wanted to kiss Milla from the moment he'd first seen her in London, and he'd thought that he'd shown enormous restraint by waiting till the party in California.

But looking back on all this now, the thing that really bugged Ed was the super-lame way he'd let Harry move in on this beautiful girl. Hell. He'd been so miffed and jealous about his younger brother's smooth manoeuvres that he hadn't even tried to reconnect with Milla after that party.

He'd been too dumb to pick up the underlying promise in her kiss, and he'd simply stepped out of the picture. Let her go.

He'd never dreamed that she'd floated around in the party scene for weeks before anything happened with Harry.

What an idiot he'd been. A total klutz. The world's biggest fool. He'd deserved to lose her.

Now, exhausted after a night of remorse, Ed lay watching the first shimmers of morning light. A rooster crowed somewhere in the distance. A car motor started up. Small birds chirped in the tree outside the bakery window. And some of Ed's gloom evaporated.

He knew things were supposed to look better in the morning, and now, with the coming of daylight, he realised that perhaps he could salvage one or two positives from this disaster.

For starters, he now knew that he hadn't imagined the heady passion and heart-lifting wildness of that long-remembered kiss. Call it male ego, but it was a relief to know that Milla's frightened withdrawal afterwards hadn't been entirely his fault.

But this was only a minor consolation, especially now that his feelings for her were growing stronger every minute that he spent with her. After this short weekend, he wasn't just fighting a longing to make love to her. He was beginning to wish he could be part of her life, wanted to make her part of his.

Wanted to throw off their pasts and start afresh.

But that wasn't going to happen. There was no point in wishing they still had a chance. Milla had made her feelings about his family very clear. And she was totally justified.

And if Ed was honest, he had little confidence that he could provide her with the happy-ever-after she wanted, the kind of secure, stable marriage that her friends Heidi and Brad enjoyed. As Milla was only too aware, Cavanaugh men were incapable of providing long-term happiness for their wives.

Ed didn't like to lump himself in the same bracket as his brother and his father, but the sad truth was his longest relationship had lasted six months. Caro, his latest girlfriend, would soon join the others who'd tired of the long hours he worked.

He supposed his main virtue was that he hadn't complicated things by marrying any of those women. But was that really a virtue? Truth was, he'd never been prepared to make promises with his heart. There were times he wasn't even sure that he had one.

Even if he tried to explain any of this to Milla, he couldn't expect her to trust him. Too much had gone wrong for her. She'd married his brother, and his brother had treated her dreadfully. And then, in the midst of heartbreak and separation, she'd lost their baby.

Now, with admirable courage and determination, Milla was digging her own way out of the emotional wreckage. She was finding her own version of happiness. What had she called it? Self-worth.

Free of Cavanaugh contamination.

If she ever contemplated another relationship, she would want a guy she could trust implicitly, and a guy who shared her values—like this self-worth idea.

Ed mulled that over again now. He knew he was trustworthy, but he was pretty damn sure he'd score low on any measure of personal satisfaction.

He wasn't sure if he'd ever truly liked himself.

And yet, if he tried to recall any moments of deep happiness and satisfaction in his life, his mind winged straight back to Michigan. He saw himself as a boy, bringing fresh farm eggs into his grandmother's kitchen, and he remembered the way she had loved him. Looking back, Ed knew that she hadn't loved him because of the exams he'd passed with flying colours, or the races he'd won, or the teams he'd captained.

She'd loved him simply because he was her grandson. Around her, he'd always felt good about himself.

His grandfather had shown him a similar brand of simple, uncomplicated love. Ed could remember standing beside the old man and looking up at the barn they'd painted—the gleaming red walls, bright and solid against a clear blue autumn sky.

'We did a good job, Ed. That's going to last your grandmother and me for years. Might even see us out.'

Ed could still remember the love shining in his grandfather's eyes, could remember the feel of his knobbly hand giving his shoulder an affectionate squeeze.

Self-worth. He'd felt it then. Even in small doses it could make a difference. A huge difference.

Of course, he'd felt it on occasions as an adult, when he'd worked late into the night to pull off a business coup. Yeah, he was proud of the way he'd steered Cavanaugh Enterprises safely through the stresses and dangers of the recent global financial crises. But that sense of satisfaction was hard to hang onto when he came home each night to an empty apartment.

That was the thing about self-worth—it wasn't only about achievement. It was about making connections with people who mattered.

He'd had glimpses of that in the past couple of days, when he'd experienced the heady elation of painting these bakery walls with Milla…when he'd looked up from the laptop and seen her smile, and again when small chubby fingers had pushed pieces of cucumber onto the side of his plate…

This morning, damn it, Ed couldn't help wondering—just for argument's sake—if fate offered him half a chance to share his life with Milla, would he grab it? Should he?

Could he, in all conscience, be certain that he wouldn't stuff it up for her again?

After the night's revelations, Milla was a little nervous as she descended the stairs for breakfast. She breathed a little easier when she saw that Ed was already up and dressed and busy making coffee.

His manner as he greeted her was friendly but cautious, giving her the impression that he was as worried as she was about overstepping boundaries. Relieved, Milla accepted the mug he handed her and joined him to sit on the back steps in the sun while they drank their coffee.

The steps weren't wide, so she was way too conscious of her proximity to Ed's massive shoulders, too conscious of every part of Ed, actually. To distract herself, she waxed lyrical about her plans for the long narrow strip of tangled backyard that stretched in front of them.

'I know it's only a weedy mess at the moment, but it faces north, so it's perfect for growing vegetables.' She waved her hand, pointing. 'I'll put the veggie plot right in the middle with pavers down the centre. And I want to make a courtyard here at the bottom of these steps, and I'll get a table and chairs for alfresco dining, and—'

'Hang on,' interrupted Ed, with a grin. 'How do you plan to make the courtyard?'

'With stone pavers.'

His eyes widened, and he looked both amused and surprised. 'You? On your own?'

'Why not?' Milla responded airily. 'Pick up any gardening magazine and you'll find instructions.' Before Ed could pin her down on the engineering details of her courtyard, Milla hurried on. 'I want to leave sections between the pavers for growing herbs and I'll have a chook pen at the far end. And I'll plant nasturtiums. Lots of lovely, bright nasturtiums. They're so ordinary, but they always cheer me.'

Ed was watching her now with a smile that held a hint of disturbing sadness. 'You're really looking forward to all of this, aren't you?'

Puzzled by his reaction, Milla gave a shrug. 'It'll have to be a long-term project. The bakery will have to come first, but I'll tackle the yard in stages.'

'You want to make a start this morning?'

Milla gave a laughing shake of her head. 'Heavens, no, Ed. And I wasn't telling you about this in the hope that you'll help me. I'm not your responsibility.' She was pleased that she said this quite firmly.

She still felt thrown by Ed's willingness to help. Until he'd turned up on her doorstep, she'd only ever seen him in business suits that were imported from Milan and came with five-thousand-dollar price tags. Since he'd been here, he'd slept on a stretcher, he'd helped her with her painting and her business plan, but she couldn't possibly ask him to dig up long grass and weeds.

'I think you've earned a day off,' she said emphatically.

Attractive lines fanned from the corners of his eyes as he smiled at her. 'Will you take the day off with me?'

It was the worst moment to blush, but he was sitting so close she could almost feel his body heat, and now as he posed his invitation his grey eyes held a sparkle that lit flashpoints all over her.

'What—what would you like to do?' She looked away as she spoke, in case she blushed again.

'There's a farm near here. I read about it while I was doing the research for your business plan and I saw that they have a display section that's open to the public on weekends.'

Milla frowned. 'Since when have you been interested in farms?'

'This one grows organic wheat. Spelt and other heirloom varieties.' Ed gave a smiling shrug. 'I thought you might be curious. I know there's a growing interest worldwide in organic products. It's not just trendy. There are all kinds of benefits—both for health and economics.'

'That's true. I must admit I've toyed with the idea of making spelt bread.'

Ed was already jumping to his feet. 'Let's go, then.' He held out his hand to help her up.

* * *

It turned into one of those standout days that Milla knew she would remember for ever. A sunny winter's day with the clearest of blue skies and air as sparkling as champagne.

They drove to the spelt farm and Ed spent a surprising amount of time talking to the farmer, asking technical questions about soil and rainfall requirements and the various uses for these crops, including their benefits as stockfeed.

Afterwards, they enjoyed a picnic lunch on the banks of Bellaroo Creek, dining on a loaf of olive bread that she'd baked the day before. They ate it with slices of pecorino cheese and pickled mushrooms and, when they'd finished, they rolled up the bottoms of their jeans and paddled like children in the pretty, clear-running creek.

Milla collected several beautifully smooth, water-washed stones, including a round, smooth piece of red glass.

'I'll put these in a jar on a window sill,' she said, when she showed them to Ed. 'They'll look lovely with the sun shining through them.'

With a thoughtful frown, he picked the piece of red glass from her hand and held it up to the sun, making it glow like an expensively cut ruby.

'Don't you love it when ordinary things are suddenly stunning?' she said. 'A kind of accidental beauty.'

Ed's response was a lopsided smile, but his eyes were so shiny Milla felt a strange ache in her arms. As if she wanted to hold him.

The ache lingered as they sat on the creek bank again, letting their feet dry in the sun.

After a bit, Ed lay back, stacking his hands under his head. 'Forgive me,' he said, staring up through the overhead branches. 'But there's something I don't quite get about you, Milla. I mean, here you are, fitting back into life in the country so easily. And it seems right for you. But it makes me wonder why you took up with Harry, why you let yourself be sucked into the Beverly Hills set.'

'I know.' Milla felt suddenly cold and she hugged her jacket closer. 'When I look back now, I find it hard to understand, too. But we all make mistakes when we're young, don't we? I was hell-bent on getting away and breaking the mould. I suppose I was rebelling, like most young people do. I wanted to be the exact opposite of my parents.'

'Didn't happen that way for me,' Ed said quietly.

'No, you've followed in your father's footsteps.'

'Hoping for his approval.' The hard edge in Ed's voice was at odds with the sadness in his eyes.

Milla felt her heart go out to him. 'Gerry's a difficult man to please.'

'Yeah, just ask his three wives.' Ed grimaced as he said this and he sat up swiftly, leaned forward, propping his elbows on his bent knees.

Milla thought how at home he looked in this bush setting, dressed in a simple T-shirt and casual jeans. She liked the unpretentious way Ed seemed to live in his powerful body as if he was completely unaware of its charms. So different from Harry.

'So what would you like to do now?' he asked.

I'd like to lie here in the sun while you kiss me.

The longing was so strong she almost said the words aloud.

When she remained silent, Ed turned to her and the smouldering grey of his eyes stole her breath.

For a moment, neither of them spoke. It was happening all over again, Milla thought. That spectacular rush of awareness they'd first sensed in London.

But then, with an angry-sounding sigh, Ed got to his feet. And the moment was gone.

'Let's go back,' he said. 'And finish your painting.'

A tense silence hung over them as they drove back to Bellaroo Creek. Ed did his best to stay calm, but he was shaking inside. There'd been a critical moment on that creek bank when he'd nearly pulled Milla into his arms and played out every fantasy that had plagued him since he'd arrived here.

Now, he had to ask himself why he'd stayed this extra day, taking a drive in the country and talking to farmers and paddling in creeks. He'd come here to help Milla with her business and, instead, he'd distracted her, and he'd damn well nearly made a prize fool of himself.

Again.

For the rest of the evening, he would concentrate on practical matters. He would make sure there was nothing more he could do for Milla. For her *business.*

Tomorrow morning he would leave and no doubt they would both say goodbye with a huge sense of relief.

Milla woke to the ping of a message landing on her mobile phone. She yawned and rolled over, rubbed at her eyes and saw pale white light showing beyond the window curtains. It was too early to get up, she decided quickly. She would have enough of early mornings once the bakery opened.

Shivering, she settled back into her pillows and pulled the covers up again. The message on her phone could wait.

But just as she was comfortable another ping sounded. Milla frowned. This was unusual. Since returning to Australia, she rarely got messages, let alone two in quick succession. Could it be her parents?

Fear flared as her mind raced through possibilities. Her mother or father had taken ill during their Mediterranean cruise. They'd lost their passports. A car bomb had exploded in one of the ports—Turkey or Northern Africa.

Having thoroughly alarmed herself now, Milla leapt up and grabbed her phone. There were three missed calls, but they weren't from anyone in her address book, so that was a relief. It was probably a spammer, but just to be sure she checked for a voice message.

'Hi, Milla,' said a woman with an American accent. 'It's Sarah Goldman. I'm trying to contact Ed Cavanaugh. If you know where he is, could you please ask him to call me asap? It's urgent. Thanks.'

Milla stared at her phone in surprise, as if somehow it could provide answers. She remembered Sarah Goldman, Ed's PA. They'd met at a couple of the Cavanaugh gatherings Harry had been forced to attend.

Why hadn't Sarah rung Ed directly?

Milla glanced at the time. It was almost seven. She thought about dashing straight downstairs in her nightie—this was urgent, Sarah Goldman had said. But after a night of dreams featuring Ed in the starring role, she quickly retracted that option.

She hurried through to the bathroom instead, washed her face and ran a brush through her hair. Her curls bounced back stronger each day now that she'd given up the bleach and the straighteners. She liked what she saw in the mirror. It was like rediscovering her true self again.

Back in her bedroom, she pulled on jeans and a sweater that was the exact same shade of grey as Ed's eyes. *Stop it. Stop thinking about him every waking moment.* She shoved her feet into sheepskin slippers, picked up her phone and headed downstairs.

As she expected, Ed was still in his sleeping bag, although he couldn't have been asleep, because he rolled out as soon as he heard her coming, and he was on his feet by the time she reached the bottom of the stairs.

He was dressed in track pants and a T-shirt. His jaw was dark with a five o'clock shadow and his hair was rumpled and messy. He looked unforgivably sexy.

He sent her a sleepy smile. 'Good morning.'

Even his voice was deeper and sexier at this hour.

'Morning.' Milla forced a cheerful smile. 'I was woken by a phone call. Someone's looking for you. Sarah Goldman.'

'Sarah rang *you*?' Ed asked, frowning.

Milla held out her phone. 'She left a message asking you to call her as soon as possible. I've no idea how she found my number.'

'Sarah's a very efficient PA. Better than a bloodhound at tracking me down.' Ed sighed, ran a hand through his hair, making it even messier. 'What the hell's happened?'

He looked as if he hadn't had nearly enough sleep. 'I turned off my phone when I came out here. I wanted to take the weekend off. Obviously it was a *bad* mistake.' Bending quickly, he extracted his BlackBerry from a pocket in his travel bag, frowned at it as he waited for the messages to load.

'I'll start the coffee,' Milla volunteered.

Ed grunted his thanks, without shifting his gaze from the small screen. Then he grimaced, clearly not liking what he saw. Almost immediately, he began to swear. Loudly.

Milla knew it would be begging the obvious to ask if he had a problem, but as she busied herself fixing the coffee she hoped his problem wasn't too serious. After Harry's recent death, she was sure Ed needed a break from bad news.

The news had to be pretty bad, though, judging by the fury in Ed's face as he read his messages, and the string of oaths he continued to let fly.

'I can't believe it,' he groaned. 'Cleaver freaking Holdings. The lying weasels. After the way I bent over backwards to help them last year.'

'So it's a business issue?' Milla couldn't help asking.

Ed looked as if he wanted to hurl the phone into the wall. 'Cleaver's started a hostile takeover.'

Milla had only a vague idea what this meant. She knew the Cavanaughs had floated their company on the stock market a few years ago, but Harry had never been very interested in the business, and she'd been too absorbed with their personal problems to pay it much attention.

Throwing up his hands in despair, Ed paced to the end of the bakery, let out another, louder groan and marched back.

With an air of desperation, he held out the phone to her. 'Cleaver filed a bid for a majority chunk of our stock late on Friday afternoon. It was already Saturday here and I'd turned this damn thing off. They were trying to steal my company while I was out of the country.' He ground the words out between tightly gritted teeth.

Milla felt helpless, but she had to ask. 'Can they get away with that?'

Ed scowled. 'Not if I can help it.'

Even as he said this she could see his mind clearing its initial anger and making plans.

'I have no idea what time it is in the US, but I'll get onto Sarah,' he said more calmly. 'I know she'll answer the phone even if it's two a.m. I'll have to call a few others, as well, but Sarah will give me the latest and she can book me on the first flight home.'

'I can book you a flight.'

Ed's eyes flashed a brief, appreciative smile. 'Thanks, but it's OK. Sarah's used to this. She'll do it in a flash.' Then he was scowling again. 'I'll have to leave for Sydney straight away. Damn it. I wish it wasn't five hours away.' He shot Milla a sharp glance. 'I don't suppose I can fly from here?'

Ed was back to being a business executive, back to his true calling. But Milla knew he must be desperately worried, too. Everything that was important to him could quite possibly be slipping from beneath him. She was surprised by how much this saddened her.

'There's an airport at Parkes,' she said. 'I'll ring and find out about flights.'

'That'd be great. I'll hire a plane. A private jet. A milk crate. As long as it has wings. Anything that can fly me to Sydney.'

'I'm onto it.'

The next fifteen minutes were a whirlwind with both

Ed and Milla on separate phones, at times calling questions to each other as they sorted and settled bookings.

Incredibly, they achieved the impossible, finding flights for Ed that would take him from Parkes to Sydney in time to link up with an international departure direct to JFK in New York.

'How's your father handling this?' Milla asked once everything was settled.

Ed pulled a face. 'He's volcanic, as you'd expect. Blaming me for taking my eye off the ball.'

Before Milla could respond, Ed said, 'Don't worry about breakfast. Coffee will be fine,' and then he disappeared upstairs for a hasty shower and shave.

She felt slightly dazed by all the sudden busyness after the laid-back, relaxed mood of yesterday. When Ed came downstairs again, he looked suddenly too neat with his beard gone and his wet hair slicked back.

'At least I got your business plan sorted yesterday,' he said as Milla handed him his coffee.

'Yes, and I'm incredibly grateful.' But she felt bad, too. If Ed hadn't stayed here to write a plan for her little, unimportant business, his own VIP business might not be in trouble. She knew he would hate to see his company taken over, and now he had to fight for its independence. 'I just hope everything works out for you.'

He nodded unhappily, took another swig of coffee.

She couldn't believe how bleak she felt now that Ed was about to hurry out of her life finally and for ever.

'While you finish your coffee, I'll just check upstairs,' she said, worried that she was about to cry in front of him. 'I'll make sure you haven't left anything.'

There was only the bathroom to check, of course, and Ed had already brought his zipper bag with shaving gear down, but at least Milla had an excuse to splash water on her face, which would hopefully help to keep the tears at bay.

She was drying her face when she looked down and saw the little brush on the floor. It didn't belong to her, but it didn't look like something Ed would own either. It was an old-fashioned shaving brush with a blue and cream ceramic handle and proper bristles. Picking it up, she saw the words *Made in England* printed on the bottom.

She hurried back down, holding the brush in her curled palm and liking the solid, non-plastic feel of it.

'I think you forgot this, Ed. It was in the bathroom.' She held the brush out to him.

He looked surprised, but pleased.

When she handed it over their fingers made contact, and she felt the zap of a small lightning flash.

'Thanks,' he said. 'I wouldn't want to lose this.' For the first time this morning his brow cleared and his expression softened. 'I don't use it much, but it was my grandfather's. I guess it's just a kind of—'

'Keepsake?' she suggested.

He smiled at her. 'Yes. An important keepsake.'

'I'm glad I found it, then.'

'Yeah.' Ed ran his thumb over the soft bristles and for a moment he seemed lost in thought. Then he unzipped his pack and slipped the little brush inside. 'I've kept it as a kind of reminder of the old guy. I—I guess I wanted to be like him.'

When he straightened again, he gave a small, self-deprecating smile. 'But I don't really know why I've kept it. I've paid no attention. I've gone my own way.'

Milla said softly, 'You might be more like him than you realise.'

Ed looked at her for a long moment and he gave her a slow, sad smile. 'I'll hold that thought.'

A huge lump filled her throat and her heart was heavy as she walked outside with him into the cold morning. This was the second time she'd farewelled Ed from Bellaroo Creek, and she'd felt sad enough last time.

This time she'd discovered how deeply she cared for him and the knowledge caused a horrible, aching weight in her chest. She felt fearful for Ed, too, as if she were sending him off to an unknown battlefield.

'There's so much I have to thank you for, Ed. You came back here with the equipment. You helped me with painting the walls and with the business plan. And if you hadn't come—'

To her surprise, Ed silenced her by pressing a finger to her lips. 'If I hadn't come, we wouldn't have had that very important conversation, and I would never have understood what went wrong with our first date.'

He no longer seemed in a hurry as he traced the shape of her chin with the backs of his fingers. 'Believe me, Milla, I have no regrets.'

Her heart was pounding now. She tried to tell herself not to be foolish. Ed was a Cavanaugh. She should be glad he was going back to where he belonged.

But she'd seen such a different side to him this weekend. Against her better judgement, despite everything she knew about his family, she'd fallen for him again. 'I hope everything works out for you.'

Ed smiled. 'Thanks.' He didn't step away.

Now he was framing her face with his big hands,

holding her just so, and looking into her eyes. 'Good luck with everything.'

'You, too.'

He kissed her then. Just the loveliest kiss, sweet but incredibly intimate, and as Milla kissed him back, softly, gently, she handed him her heart, gift-wrapped, with his name on it.

The kiss was over far too quickly. Time was running out, and Ed had to leave.

'You'll do well here,' he said, flashing a quick glance around the bakery. 'Let me know when you have a date for the opening.'

She knew he wouldn't be back, but she said, 'I will, yes.' Her throat was so choked she could barely get the words out, and her eyes filled with tears. 'I hope every-thing works out for you and the business.'

She thought she saw a damp sheen in his eyes, but he turned away quickly, hurried around the ute, and jumped into the driver's seat.

This time, she didn't stand on the footpath to watch him drive off. There wasn't much point when she was blinded by tears.

CHAPTER NINE

ED DIDN'T WASTE a precious minute of the two hours he had to spend in the international departure lounge before his plane took off. When he wasn't receiving or making phone calls to the other side of the world, he used the time to prepare letters that would be emailed first thing in the morning to Cavanaugh Enterprise's shareholders.

Ed had to persuade their investors against selling their shares to the Cleaver group, despite the tempting, above-market prices that Cleaver was offering.

He felt sick at the thought of their company collapsing, of their employees in danger of losing their jobs. Fortunately, he and his father had established a supermajority clause when they'd floated the business on the stock market, and this meant that eighty per cent of shareholders had to approve any acquisition. Now, Ed desperately needed those eighty per cent on his side.

Sitting in the business lounge, he was oblivious to other passengers as he worked hard at rewriting and refining the message he would send out, searching for exactly the right words. He had to find the perfect, delicate balance that would appeal to his investors' emotions as well as their hard business heads.

At least, there was one good thing in the midst of this disaster—the concentrated work kept his mind off Milla.

Almost.

But there were moments when Ed caved. No matter how hard he tried to resist the temptation, his thoughts flew back to their goodbye kiss, and every time he thought about it he felt echoes of the kiss reverberate inside him like a quivering bowstring after the arrow was released. The simple kiss had been so powerful, had caught him completely off guard.

He hadn't planned to kiss Milla, but everything had unravelled from the moment he touched her. A simple touch to the soft bloom of her cheek had carried such a high voltage, and a man couldn't touch a girl like her without wanting to kiss her.

From the moment their lips touched, her response was so sweet and tender. So apparently innocent and, yet, so potent, as if they'd exchanged a secret message they dared not speak aloud.

Or was he reading too much into it?

Yeah. Surely he was getting carried away?

Damn it, when had he become such a hopeless romantic? There was every chance Milla was happy to see the back of him.

Honestly, it was probably just as well that he'd had no choice but to leave her. As his father had so angrily accused, Ed had taken his eye off the ball for one weekend, and now he was in danger of losing everything that mattered, not just to him but to everyone who worked for him. Cavanaugh's employees and their families relied on him now, more than ever.

He was relieved when his boarding call was finally announced. He wasn't looking forward to the ten-thousand-mile journey, but he was anxious to get back to New York, to get his business problems sorted. And putting distance between himself and Bellaroo Creek would no doubt provide much needed emotional perspective as well.

As his plane took off over the red roofs of Sydney, over the spectacular harbour and the sparkling beaches, he took his last view of Australia.

It was time to realign his priorities.

Mrs Jones beamed at Milla as she came into the general store with a large cane basket on each arm.

'What have you brought for us today?' the store-keeper asked as she rubbed her plump hands in glee-ful expectation.

'Two more samples,' Milla told her. 'Whole-grain bread rolls and vanilla slices.'

'Vanilla slices?' Mrs Jones gave a rapturous sigh and dramatically pressed her hands against her heart. 'I can't remember the last time I ate a vanilla slice. I sup-pose it must have been before your parents left town.'

'Everyone mentions my parents. I'm starting to feel the pressure,' Milla said with a rueful smile. 'Fingers crossed my slices are up to scratch.'

Mrs Jones lifted a corner of the pink gingham tea towel covering one of the baskets and she grinned broadly. 'Ooh, these smell divine and they look per-fect.' She gave Milla a fond, almost motherly smile. 'I'm sure you have nothing to worry about, my dear.'

Turning, she called over her shoulder, lifting her voice to reach her husband, who was busy unpack-ing groceries at the back of the store. 'Bob, come here quickly. Come and take a look at this. You'll never guess what Milla's brought in for us today.'

Milla laughed. 'I hope the rest of the district will be as enthusiastic as you guys.'

'Oh, they are already, Milla. Believe you me. Everyone's talking about your bakery.'

'Well, I'm very grateful to you for helping me to spread the word.'

It had been such a coup when the Joneses had happily agreed to sell samples of Milla's goods in their store throughout the lead-up to the bakery's official opening. To the Joneses' and Milla's mutual delight, the experiment seemed to be paying off.

Not only were Milla's baked goods selling well, but word was spreading. As an added bonus, this marketing strategy had also given her the perfect opportunity to sort out which products were most popular with her potential customers.

In fact, all her plans were coming together beautifully. Since the council had given their final approval, Milla's project had steamrolled ahead. She'd finished painting the shop and the workroom, and she'd set up the baking equipment, working out the most efficient positioning of each item in terms of time and motion. She'd placed orders for bulk quantities of flour and sugar and yeast.

She'd also experimented with recipes for bread, pies, cakes and slices, and she'd made careful notes of timing and quantities. Successes and failures.

Most recently, Milla had placed ads in the bakery's window as well as in the general store, and soon she would be interviewing the applicants who'd responded to the two positions she wanted to fill. She was looking for someone friendly and outgoing to help with shop-front sales, and another person, possibly a teenager, to help her each morning with slicing and packing the bread.

Each day she felt a little more excited, a little more optimistic that she really could do this. And she was touched and encouraged by the number of people who had popped into the bakery to give her the thumbs-up, and to tell her how much they were looking forward to opening day. Already, before the shop opened, she was beginning to feel a part of the town once again.

Now, Mrs Jones positioned Milla's baskets on the counter close to the cash register, and said with a coy smile, 'I don't suppose that nice American fellow will be coming back for the opening?'

Milla's heart thudded at the mere mention of Ed, even though this question was getting monotonous. Almost every day, there'd been someone in this tiny township who seemed to know about Ed. Inevitably they would slip a not-so-subtle question or comment about the nice American fellow who'd made such a stir during his all too brief stay.

Milla was trying really, really hard not to think about Ed. She'd exchanged a couple of emails with him, and he'd told her that he had strategies in place to avert the initial thrust of the takeover threat. He was hopeful that Cavanaugh Enterprises would remain intact.

He'd made polite enquiries about the bakery, which she'd answered carefully, without going too over-the-top with her enthusiasm. After their initial polite exchanges, their emails had lapsed, and she'd decided that was totally appropriate.

They had no reason to write to each other. They lived

on different continents, in different worlds with totally different lifestyles. Ed's hometown was a famous multicultural metropolis with more than eight million people while Milla's was a tiny rural town at the bottom of the world where the population had only recently crept past four hundred.

They had nothing in common... Not. A. Thing.

Apart from a couple of truly sensational kisses.

And Milla was working very hard to forget about those etched-on-her-mind events. Unfortunately, she'd been unsuccessful so far, but she would have to try harder. She didn't want anything to distract her from her goals. This was make-or-break time for her business. It was time to be strong. Time to focus on her preparation and planning.

Of course, now that Mrs Jones had thrown her the difficult question, she was watching Milla carefully as she waited for her answer. Somehow, Milla managed to smile just as she had every other time she'd faced this question.

'Ed won't be coming back,' she assured the storekeeper, and, like all the other times she'd said this, she felt a little chunk of her heart chip off and fall away.

Gerry Cavanaugh stood at the plate-glass window in Ed's penthouse office, grim-faced, hands sunk in his trouser pockets as he stared out at the skyscrapers and busy streets of Midtown Manhattan. 'So we dodged the bullet,' he said, without looking at Ed.

'Yes, it looks like we're finally in the clear.' Last night Ed had been euphoric when he'd realised that Cavanaugh Enterprises was out of danger. This morning he braced himself for the grilling he knew his father was about to deliver. After all, Gerry Cavanaugh never came to Ed's office for any other purpose than to point out his son's errors.

Still intent on the view, his father said, tightly, 'You did well, son.'

Shock erupted in Ed. In thirty-five years, this was the highest praise he'd ever received from his old man. For a moment he was too stunned to speak.

Fleetingly, he wondered if his father was all right. Could he be ill? Could this be the first signs of senility?

Ed was still reeling when Gerry turned from the window. 'But tell me this, Ed.' His voice was cooler now and yet somehow louder.

Ed's brief sense of elation fizzled and died. *Here it comes. The iron fist inside the velvet glove.*

Spearing him with his steely, ice-blue gaze, his father said, 'Why the hell did you think you were entitled to waste so much damn time in Australia?'

Ed let out his breath on a silent groan. 'Give me a break.'

'Give you a *break*? Are you for real?' Now the anger flared, as fierce and volcanic and familiar as ever. 'You took a damn break, Ed. You decided to give yourself an entire week's break, holed up in Sydney. You were supposed to be running this company and you turned your damn phone off.'

'Look, I know it was a mistake to turn off the phone.' Ed spoke quietly, in his most placating tone. He was in appeasement mode now, a role he was well and truly used to. 'I regret turning that phone off. I probably regret it more than anyone. But I wasn't having a vacation in Sydney. You know I went down there to find Milla. And when I found her, I discovered that she needed help. *Our* help. She got a raw deal from Harry. She'd lost her baby. To be honest, I was worried about—'

'I thought she rejected our help,' his father interrupted.

'Milla rejected Harry's money,' Ed said quietly and evenly. 'That's not quite the same thing.'

His father didn't look convinced.

'Another point,' Ed continued. 'Milla's not in Sydney. She's gone back to her hometown. A tiny little place in rural New South Wales.' He watched his dad with narrowed eyes. 'I thought you might understand that. After all, you grew up in a small country town.'

'I don't see how it's relevant.' But despite the snapping retort, his dad looked uncomfortable. A dark stain crept up from his shirt collar.

Ed had never really understood exactly why his father was reluctant to acknowledge his country roots. He must have had a happy childhood, growing up on the farm with loving parents, and yet, as far as Ed was aware, his dad had only gone back for one or two Thanksgivings or Christmas gatherings, and then, sadly, for his parents' funerals.

Gerry Cavanaugh had embraced the big city life and he'd poured all his energy and focus into his business. And he'd made it clear that he expected Ed, as his eldest son, to follow in his footsteps.

It wouldn't be wise to mention Milla's bakery, Ed decided now. Remembering his own reactions when he first heard about her plans, he knew he couldn't expect his father to remotely understand.

'So I assume I can trust you to stay at the helm?' His father's voice carried an all too familiar sarcastic edge now. 'There'll be no more rescue missions down under?'

'No, of course not.' Ed made a show of checking the time.

'Yes, I'm going,' his father growled. But he didn't move. He cleared his throat and looked suddenly, uncharacteristically nervous, almost red-faced. 'By the way, Ed. I guess I should tell you. I'm getting married in a couple of weeks' time.'

He didn't add the word *again*, even though this was Wife Number Four. It wasn't easy for Ed to manufacture the appropriate degree of surprised pleasure, but he managed. 'Congratulations.'

'I guess you should come to dinner,' his dad said gruffly. 'To meet Maddie.'

'Maddie?' Ed frowned. This was a new name. Last he'd heard, his father was dating a former flight attendant, half his age, called Cindy.

'Madeleine Brown. She's…a widow.'

'Right,' Ed said, intrigued. 'Thanks. I—I'd like to meet her.'

'Friday at Spiegel's, then. Eight o'clock. You'll bring Caro, I suppose?'

'Ah, no… I don't think so.' Ed dropped his gaze as he shrugged. 'There's been a parting of the ways.'

'Well, well…another one bites the dust.'

Ed was tempted to snap back that at least he hadn't made a habit of *marrying* the wrong women; he'd merely dated them. But he kept his counsel, and to his relief his father strode off, leaving him in peace.

Peace was a relative term, of course, suggesting a certain lack of restlessness. Truth to tell, Ed had been decidedly restless since his return from Australia.

He'd found the hours spent behind his desk or locked in boardrooms were ambushed by memories of that little bakery in Bellaroo Creek. All kinds of unexpected images had leapt into his focus. He would see Milla's hands, pale and distractingly graceful, even when she was busy with a rolling pin. Remembered her happy smile or her small frown of concentration as she made a lattice pattern with pastry strips over cherries.

He'd remember driving with her through the countryside in the moonlight. Her smile against a backdrop of endless fields of golden wheat. Hell, he'd even called in at a local bakery on Columbus Avenue and tried to peek out the back to see how they'd set up their machinery.

At the oddest moments, he would remember driving out to a barbecue at sunset when the sky was lavender and the wheat fields were pink and gold.

Too many times, he remembered Milla's farewell kiss, the sweetness of her lips, the soft green of her eyes, shiny with tears.

And then there was another thought, one that would have been inconceivable before he left for Australia. The thought shocked him, and he would never admit it to anyone. He could barely admit it to himself. But there were times while he was fighting to save his company when he'd wondered if the takeover would, in all honesty, be such a devastating disaster.

While Ed might have lost his job, he could have fought to save his employees'. In reality, a takeover might have left them better off. And he would have relinquished a shedload of responsibility and hard work. He would have been free to look at other options. New horizons. He'd even begun to understand why Harry had rebelled, and for the first time he was feeling less certain.

These were truly crazy thoughts, of course, and Ed had begun to wonder if the long plane journey hadn't shaken a screw loose.

Milla was standing on the footpath outside the bakery when her phone rang. 'Good morning,' she answered, smiling broadly. 'This is Bellaroo Bakery. How can I help you?'

'Hi, Milla.'

Zap!

At the sound of Ed's voice, a massive jolt almost lifted her from the ground. She had to take a calming breath before she could answer. Why was he ringing? Not another problem, surely?

'Hi, Ed.' Her heart was racing and she was breathless. 'How are you?'

'Fine, thanks. And you?'

'Terrific.' She had to stop to take another breath. 'Everything's falling nicely into place here.'

'Pleased to hear it. So what's the latest?'

'You—you want details?'

'Sure. If you have time… I'd love to hear how the bakery's shaping up.'

And, heaven help her, she wanted to tell him. 'Well… right now, I'm admiring a lovely new sign above the shop. The name's freshly painted in dark green on a cream background, and the writing's slightly curly and olde worlde. I love it.'

'Sounds neat. And you're still using the old name, Bellaroo Bakery?'

'Yes. I played around with other names. Heidi suggested Bun in the Oven, which is cute, but it reminded me too much of…' Milla swallowed uncomfortably. It still hurt to talk about the baby.

Ed made a soft sound of sympathy. 'So when's the opening day?' he asked.

'Next Monday.'

'Wow. So soon.' After a slight hesitation, Ed asked, 'Are you excited?'

'Yes, I am rather.'

'Nervous?'

She laughed. 'Very.' But before Ed could start worrying about her doing everything on her own, she hurried to reassure him. 'I've hired help, you'll be pleased to hear. I have two young mothers working half a week each, and they'll be in the shop, looking after the sales. And when they're not working, they'll be minding each other's babies.'

'OK. That sounds like a good arrangement.'

'I was thinking about someone to help with slicing and bagging, but I'm thinking I might only slice about a quarter of the loaves to begin with, and sell the others as whole loaves. I'm going for a more old-fashioned, wholesome product.'

'Yeah, I think that could work. People often associate tradition with quality.'

'That's what I'm hoping. If I need to do more slicing and bagging, I can. Sherry's young brother Ethan is interested in working for an hour in the mornings.'

'Good plan.' After a beat Ed asked, 'And who'll be helping you with the baking?'

Milla and Ed had discussed, or rather argued about, this when he was here. Even though he couldn't see her now, Milla squared her shoulders. 'I think I'll be fine on my own.'

'You *think*,' Ed said with soft emphasis.

'I *know* I'll be fine.' Now she lifted her chin.

'Those massive bags of flour won't lift themselves.'

'I'll be OK, Ed.'

'Don't forget, your mother had your father's help, Milla.'

'I'm starting on a much smaller scale.'

'That's something, I guess.'

'Please don't start trying to boss me long distance.'

'I won't. I promise.' His voice was gentle now. 'I'll just be concerned at long distance.'

Don't do that either. Forget about me. Hopeless tears stung. She said quickly, 'I thought you must have rung because you had news to share.'

'I do have news, actually. My father's getting married again.'

'Oh.' It was hard to respond to this with enthusiasm.

'I'm meeting the lucky lady tonight over dinner at Spiegel's.'

'Spiegel's? Nice. I'm treating Heidi and Brad and the kids to dinner here.'

'Sounds like fun. Say hi to them from me, won't you? You'll have a great evening.'

'I hope we will, Ed. I know it's a bit stark in the bakery, but I'll fill a few jugs with greenery and I'll have some music going. Some wine. Candles to relieve the bareness. It's really cold here at the moment, so I'm making minestrone soup and ciabatta bread.'

'You know how to make ciabatta?' He sounded incredulous.

Milla laughed. 'I've just taken a big round loaf out of the oven and it looks great. Remember when we went to that organic farm near Parkes, and I told you about the three months I spent working on an organic farm in Italy? Well, the family ended up sharing their four-hundred-year-old recipe.'

'You must have charmed them.'

'I think they were charmed by the fact that my parents were bakers. And I made them my stuffed olive bread.'

Ed's soft groan vibrated in her ear, vibrated all the way through her.

'I want to be there tonight,' he said.

I want you to be here, too.

She knew it was crazy, but she imagined Ed with her friends gathered at her table, imagined his dark, handsome face lit by a happy smile as he chatted with Heidi and Brad, as he charmed little Lucy, as his gaze met Milla's across the table.

Then reality crashed back. She sighed.

'I'll be thinking of you all,' Ed said softly, in a way that made goosebumps break out on her skin.

Don't think about us. You're making this impossible.

Tears filled her eyes and it was only as she began to swipe at them that she realised she was still standing outside her shop and people were watching her.

She hurried inside, closed the door. 'We shouldn't be talking like this, Ed.'

There was a long silence.

'You're right,' he said, and gave a heavy sigh. More abruptly, he added, 'Anyway, I have to go.'

'Thanks for calling. I hope you enjoy the dinner tonight. Pass on my best wishes to Gerry.'

'I will, thanks. And all the best to you for Monday morning. I'll have to work out the time difference so I can think of you getting up at three a.m.'

'I'm sure I'll appreciate your thoughts.'

He said goodbye.

'Goodbye, Ed. Take care.'

'You, too.'

Milla closed the phone and set it on the counter. She felt empty, like a flaking husk of wheat after the grain had been removed. Ed shouldn't have called her. He shouldn't have made her think about him, and he certainly shouldn't have let her know he was thinking about her.

It was time to forget.

She was moving on. This was supposed to be the start of her post-Cavanaugh life.

Madeleine Brown, his father's new fiancée, was sitting alone when Ed reached their table at Spiegel's.

'Your father's been delayed,' she told Ed, 'but he shouldn't be long.'

To Ed's surprise, Madeleine was older than his dad's previous wives, and not nearly as glamorous. But she had the loveliest warm brown eyes, and, despite her unruly, pepper and salt curls and her noticeable wrinkles, her smile was utterly enchanting. Ed liked her immediately.

'Call me Maddie,' she said as they shook hands.

'I'm very pleased to meet you, Maddie.'

'You won't remember me, but I've met you before, Ed.' Maddie's dark eyes held a charming twinkle. 'You were only a small boy. I was home for Thanksgiving, and I called in at your grandparents' place and met you and your mom.'

'Are you from Michigan?' Ed asked in amazement.

'Born and bred,' she responded with a smile. 'I grew up on the farm right next to your grandparents.'

Shock stole Ed's breath. He was completely blindsided. When he could eventually speak, he felt he had to clarify this astonishing news. 'Are you telling me that you and my father were neighbours?'

'Yes, Ed.' Maddie's smile was wistful now. 'I was the girl next door.'

'That's incredible.' He let out his breath on a whoosh of surprise.

'And your father asked me to marry him when I was just twenty.'

This surprise silenced Ed completely.

Maddie, however, seemed intent on sharing her story. 'I thought I'd had enough of living on an apple orchard, so, although I was sweet on Gerry, I turned him down. I'd set my sights on bigger things, you see. I headed for Grand Rapids where I managed to get work as a doctor's receptionist, and I married the doctor's son. He was a med student about to graduate.'

Ed's mind was racing, taking this in, putting two and two together. He couldn't help thinking that Maddie's departure from the farm must have prompted his father's exit to New York. His father had been in his early twenties when he secured his first job in insurance in Manhattan. After that, he'd studied hard and become an insurance broker and he'd worked even harder to build his business.

Now, tears brightened in Madeleine's eyes as she watched Ed. And the truth of her message dawned in him like a starburst.

When this woman rejected my father, he built his

empire to show her what she'd missed. Cavanaugh Enterprises was all about her.

'You're the love of my father's life,' he said softly.

Maddie nodded. 'So he tells me.' Her mouth twisted as she tried to smile, and then she pressed two fingers to her lips as if she was stopping herself from crying.

Eventually, she said, 'Human beings are strange creatures. Sometimes we spend an entire lifetime looking for happiness in all the wrong places.'

Indeed. Ed was thinking of his father's three unhappy marriages, and his throat tightened on a painful rock of emotion. 'Did Dad ask you to tell me this story?'

Maddie smiled more warmly again. 'He wanted you to know…but you know what a proud, stubborn and uptight coot he is. He couldn't bring himself to tell you.'

That would be right. His father had never been able to express his finer feelings, or to talk about emotional topics. But he must have found the courage to say the right things to Maddie.

Ed was truly amazed by the fond warmth that flooded Maddie's face as she spoke about his dad, even when she was calling him an uptight coot. She was either a very good actor or she genuinely loved the ornery old guy.

'So how did the two of you meet up again?'

'Gerry heard that my husband had died. He waited a year, and then came to Michigan to find me.'

She said this so simply, but it told Ed a great deal about the strength of his father's feelings. He felt shaken. Moved. Happy and sad at the same time.

'How do you feel about living in Manhattan?' he asked, forcing his mind to practicalities.

'Actually, we're looking for a place in Connecticut.'

Maddie held out her wrinkled, sun-spotted hands, free of nail polish. 'Gerry and I both want somewhere with a nice garden.'

'Dad wants a garden?' Ed couldn't imagine his father pruning or weeding, couldn't picture him stopping to smell the roses.

Maddie smiled. 'If you don't believe me, you can ask him. Here he comes now.'

CHAPTER TEN

'ARE YOU ABSOLUTELY sure you wouldn't like me to stay tonight? I'd be happy to hang around on the off-chance that you need help in the morning.'

It was late on Sunday afternoon, the eve of Milla's opening day, and this was the second time Heidi had offered to stay. Milla was beginning to feel bad about turning her friend down, but she knew Heidi couldn't continue to help on a regular basis, so until the business grew this was something Milla had to learn to manage on her own.

She felt confident that she was ready. She'd experimented with dough mixtures and she'd worked out her quantities for water and yeast as well as the timings and temperatures. Already, sourdough loaves were prepared and quietly proving in cane proving baskets. The pastries for the croissants were prepared and in the fridge. Huge bags of flour were lined up beside the big dough mixer. Every bakery surface and piece of equipment was scrupulously clean.

Tomorrow, as well as the sourdough, Milla would make white, wholemeal and mixed-grain bread loaves and buns. Once the bread was baked, she would make three kinds of meat pies—plain steak, steak and onion, and curry.

She'd decided that she would only make one or two sweet things each day to begin with. Opening day, chocolate brownies and fruit scrolls would be the stars.

Every time she thought about the shop filled with fragrant golden loaves, she felt excitement rise like steam inside her. She felt good about doing this. She really did. She knew deep down that a thriving bakery could be an important step in Bellaroo Creek's revival, and she truly wanted to see this town return to the happy, busy place she'd known in her childhood.

She wanted shift workers knocking on her door at six-thirty in the morning, wanted children calling in on their way home from school, hungry labourers lunching on her pies, families making her festive cakes part of their celebrations. Her goal was to see the bakery become the community anchor it had been in her parents' day.

Last week, when her parents had rung from Venice, Milla had finally told them what she was doing. Long ago, before she'd rebelled and left town, it had been their dream to have their only daughter join them in the bakery and carry on a family tradition. So it had felt weird to make this announcement all these years later.

Milla had closed her eyes and held her breath while she'd waited for their reaction, which was, admittedly, slow to come. But once her parents recovered from their shock, they told her how proud they were. They'd rung twice since to repeat this message, and when they arrived back from their cruise they were rushing straight to Bellaroo Creek to offer her any help or advice she might need.

Having her parents onside was important, but Milla also knew she had the goodwill of others in the town. She was encouraged by clear messages that the people of Bellaroo Creek wanted her business to do well. So she felt OK about this venture. Truly OK. And she finally convinced Heidi of her certainty over an afternoon cup of tea and slice of experimental brownie.

After Heidi drove off, with a wave and a final farewell hug, Milla walked around the shop, admiring the smooth, freshly painted walls and the cabinets waiting for her loaves and buns, the stack of crisp brown paper bags ready to be filled and handed over to customers. She admired the decorative terracotta urns filled with ornamental sheafs of wheat, the cane display baskets and shelves.

She smiled at the cute blackboard with a hand-painted floral frame that Heidi had given her as a 'business-warming' gift. It was typical of Heidi's clever taste and it was the perfect touch for this shop, lending it a quaint, rustic air. Milla loved it. Picking up a fresh stick of clean white chalk, she wrote up the details of her opening day specials.

I wish Ed could see all this.

This thought brought a heavy sigh. Since his departure, Ed had muscled his way into her head far too often, and every time Milla felt a sense of loss, like someone who'd lost a limb but could still feel its presence. She kept remembering Ed here—painting walls and working at her laptop, sleeping on the stretcher, or sitting on the back steps and listening to her garden plans. Remembered him kissing her so stirringly.

Don't be stupid. He's gone.

He doesn't belong here and he's not coming back.

You don't want him back. This is the start of your brand-new life.

She was free to carve a new future, and that was exactly what she wanted, so it made no sense that she found it so difficult to let go, especially when Ed had never been hers to hang onto.

Thoroughly annoyed with herself for letting these recurring thoughts spin endlessly, Milla showered and washed her hair. Then she heated leftover soup for her early supper and she carried an oversized mug and a hunk of bread upstairs and curled on her new sofa, dining on soup while she watched a little TV. She went to bed at eight-thirty, praying she wouldn't be too excited to sleep.

When the alarm rang, Milla shot out of bed quickly, remembering exactly what day this was and everything she had to do. Charged with excitement, she dressed in a flash, flew to the bathroom, and then hurried downstairs, flipping switches and filling the gleaming-clean bakery with light.

Wow, this was it. Her big day had arrived. First, a mug of tea, just to get her started, and then she'd dive into the morning's work.

She switched on the kettle and was reaching for a mug when she heard a knock on the shop's front door.

Heidi?

Milla couldn't hold back her smile as she went to open the door. It made sense that her best friend would want to be here to help her, and, of course, she would find things for Heidi to do. She could help keep the place clean, and she could help with lugging trays and carrying bread through to the shop at the front, and she could even help with filling the pie cases.

Milla was grinning as she flung the door open. 'I should have known you'd—'

Her greeting died on her lips when she saw the tall, dark American on her doorstep.

'Hi,' said Ed.

For a moment Milla couldn't move or speak. She could only stare at Ed as a gust of chilly night wind scudded into the shop.

She was dizzied by a rush of emotions. Joy and excitement. An overwhelming urge to leap into his arms.

Ed shut the door. He was dressed in jeans and a dark leather jacket and as he came in from the cold he looked slightly dishevelled and heartbreakingly handsome, like an image on a movie poster.

It felt like an age before Milla found her voice. 'You've got to stop doing this.' She was clutching at a display stand for support, still shaking inside. 'You can't keep turning up on my doorstep when I think you're on the other side of the world.'

'I had to come,' he said as if that were all the explanation she needed.

She gave a dazed shake of her head. 'But I was talking to you on the phone just a couple of days ago. If you were planning to come back, you could have told me.'

'It was spontaneous.' He dropped his duffle bag beside the counter.

Milla still didn't understand. The Ed Cavanaugh she'd known in the past wasn't impetuous. He was careful. He was a planner. She frowned at him. 'Why didn't you ring me?'

'To be honest, I didn't want you talking me out of

this.' With a boyish smile, he shrugged out of his jacket and began rolling up his sleeves. 'I know how fiercely independent you are.' He gave a smiling shrug. 'But now that I'm here, I'm hoping you'll let me help.'

So Ed had arrived, like the cavalry in the old Westerns that her dad used to watch. He'd come to help her.

It meant he cared. For a heady moment, Milla felt her spirits shoot sky high. It was as if the sun had come out already and was shining vibrantly, brightening the long, busy day ahead of her.

But despite her excitement and joy, she was confused. Very confused, actually. And scared that she was merely some kind of intriguing amusement for Ed.

'Don't tell me you've come all this way to help with a few bread rolls and hot pies?' she challenged.

'Why not?' he said, still smiling. 'And I'm here to lift those twenty-five-kilo bags of flour.' His grey eyes gleamed. 'There's other stuff on the go that I need to tell you, but that can keep for now.'

Milla had no idea what the 'other stuff' might be, but the reality was she didn't have time to stand around chatting. She turned her thoughts to practicalities. 'You must be exhausted after your long international flight and driving out here.'

'I arrived a few hours ago and slept in the car. I'm not tired.' His teeth flashed white as he grinned. 'I'm still functioning on New York time. So just tell me when and where you need those flourbags lifted.'

She was torn between an urge to hug him and a strong desire to hit him. She did neither. She had a bakery to open in a few hours' time and Ed was right—his explanations would have to wait.

In the workroom behind them, the kettle was boiling

furiously. 'I'm making tea,' she said, and she hurried back to it and began to pour the hot water into her mug.

Ed followed. 'I'll look after my own coffee.'

'OK.'

OK. OK. Stay calm.

Milla took a sip of hot, strong tea and felt a little steadier. Already, Ed had found the coffee and the pot and he was helping himself.

And it was almost as if he'd never left.

Stop wondering why he's here. Don't get carried away with fantasies. Concentrate on the job.

Preparation and precision timing were the key elements of successful baking. Throwing off her slightly dazed feeling, Milla checked her carefully composed timetable, then measured the yeast and the water she would need. 'OK, Mr Muscles, you can tip the first bag of flour into the dough mixer whenever you're ready.'

Ed certainly made it look easy, and it occurred to her that his big powerful shoulders were designed for physical activity, rather than for hunching over a computer.

Once the hum of the mixer started up, and the flours and water began to combine, transforming quickly into a smooth dough that the mixer continued to roll and stretch, Milla began to relax. The morning was under way.

When the dough was ready, it had to be divided, and moved into the steam prover to rise. That done, Milla set a big pot of simmering beef for the pies on the stovetop, and then worked on shaping the croissants.

To her surprise, Ed's presence wasn't a problem. He was ever-ready to help and quick to pick up on the briefest instructions and, while he didn't have the knack of working with the dough, he could wield a knife and made a fair fist of adding slits in the top of sourdough and bloomer loaves.

He was also happy to help when a bench needed to be covered with flour for kneading and shaping, or when it had to be cleaned again. And he was quick to respond when Milla wanted tins or trays set out, or collected to be carried to the ovens.

His interest and enjoyment in the whole process surprised her. Even more surprising was the fact that, despite Ed's need for instruction, he didn't get in the way, or slow her down, and it was fun to have a partner helping to share the load, especially when that partner's smile made her feel as if she were floating.

But still the questions nagged at her. Why was he here? Really? How long did he plan to stay this time? Could she cope with another fleeting visit from a man whose mere presence sent her heart spinning to the moon and back?

By six-thirty, the first loaves were coming out of the huge, hot oven. First out were the round brown sourdough loaves, followed by the traditional rectangles of white and wholemeal bread, and then the country grains, which Milla had shaped into bloomer-style loaves. They looked perfect and the place smelled sensational!

'They look good enough to eat,' Ed announced with a wink and a triumphant grin as he donned gloves and hefted a huge tray of loaves, ready to carry them through to the shop.

He shot Milla a quick, searching smile. 'You want to supervise where they go on the shelves?'

And that was another thing. Ed understood and shared her excitement, but he was also careful not to overstep the mark. He acknowledged her place as owner and boss.

Now, Milla grinned back at him, and she might have hugged him if his arms weren't laden with hot trays. As she followed Ed through to the shop, she was practically dancing with relief and excitement.

By a quarter to eight, the shelves and baskets were filled with produce and the first customers were already lining up as Heather arrived to work behind the counter.

Milla longed to watch the sale of her first loaf, but she still had too much to do. The meat for the pies had cooled in shallow trays in the fridge and now, with the pastry ready, she laid the strapped pie tins out.

'You can help with this,' she told Ed. 'I'm going to spread the pastry over the tins, and the best way to press it down is with your hands, like this,' she said, demonstrating. 'Then if you get a plastic glove, you can help put handfuls of meat into each pie.'

When they'd finished this, Ed helped Milla to lift another big roll of pastry for the pie tops. They stretched this over the entire line-up, and because the edges of the tins were sharp the pressure of the rolling pin was enough to separate each pie. And they were ready for the oven.

Milla couldn't believe how hard Ed worked, approaching each task with an almost boyish enthusiasm that was contagious. Her energy felt boundless, and while she worked the customers came in a steady stream.

And so the first day rolled happily on.

It was mid-afternoon when Ed hit the wall. As they began to give the workroom a final clean-up Milla could see the exhaustion in his face.

'Go upstairs,' she ordered him, shooing him briskly towards the stairs. 'Put your feet up. Now. Go on, before you drop.'

'I should book into the pub.'

'You can worry about the pub later. I've bought a sofa, and you're welcome to use it, or—or feel free to collapse on my bed.' She didn't look at him as she said this. The mere mention of *my bed* in Ed's presence sent an infusion of heat shooting along her veins like a fast-acting drug. Making eye contact with him would have been a dead giveaway.

It was almost dark when Ed woke, and he took a moment or two to remember where he was. He saw his boots and belt on the floor, a small television screen on a low bookcase, his duffle bag by the door.

The airline tags on the bag brought everything back—his long flight from New York and the drive out to Bellaroo Creek from Sydney, the exhilarating morning.

These were the rooms above Milla's bakery.

When a slight creak sounded, he knew it was the bathroom door opening. A moment later, Milla appeared in the doorway with a towel wrapped around her.

It was then that Ed remembered that the only route from the bathroom to Milla's bedroom was through this small sitting room. Knowing she would hate to be caught out, he quickly closed his eyes, feigning sleep.

At least…he *almost* closed his eyes, but not quite. Only a man in a coma could resist taking a good long peek at Milla Brady wearing nothing but a towel.

She had wound her coppery hair into a knot on top of her head and secured it with a tortoiseshell clip, giving him a perfect view of her pale, graceful neck and shoulders. The towel reached mid-thigh, so there was also a good deal of her bare, shapely legs on display. An added bonus was the hint of her delicious curves beneath the towel. Her skin looked so smooth and pale his fingers ached to touch.

Miraculously, he found the self-restraint to stay perfectly still on the couch. He wanted this woman, wanted to make her his, but he had to play his cards very carefully. It didn't matter that he was going mad with wanting her—he'd promised himself that he wouldn't rush. She was too important to him. He understood her fears now, and he couldn't risk scaring her off.

When Milla was halfway across the room, however, Ed realised that she'd stopped and had turned his way. And she just stood there as if she was looking down at him. With his eyes closed, he couldn't see her next move, but the room was so quiet he could hear his own breathing, and it wasn't exactly calm.

He sensed Milla coming closer, bringing with her the lingering scent of the jasmine soap she'd used in the shower.

He opened his eyes.

Damn it, he had to.

'Oh!' Instinctively, Milla clutched the towel she'd knotted over her breasts, and a bright pink blush spread from her neck to her cheeks.

'What time is it?' Ed asked with a theatrical yawn.

'Ah—around five-thirty. In the afternoon.' She looked delightfully embarrassed. A blushing Botticelli vision in an apricot and white striped towel.

'I went for a run,' she said, her green eyes round and serious, as if it was important that he understood exactly why she was here. 'If I want to stay on top of this new workload, I need to keep fit. And—and then after the run, I had a shower.'

She was talking quickly to cover her nervousness. And yet, Ed noticed with deep fascination, she didn't scuttle away like a startled crab. She didn't rush to her bedroom and slam the door on him. And while he knew he had to take this carefully, Ed had no intention of lying down when his heart's desire was a breath away.

Slowly, purposefully, he got to his feet. To his intense relief, Milla didn't step back from him.

Milla couldn't have moved, even if she'd wanted to. She was mesmerised by the sight of Ed lying there on her sofa, and she would defy any girl not to take a closer look at such masculine perfection.

She had feasted her eyes with a top-to-toe inspection, starting with Ed's thick dark hair, untidily awry, his eyelashes, dark and sooty against his cheeks, the sexy rock-star stubble on his grainy jaw.

She admired his broad shoulders stretching the thin fabric of his T-shirt, and the lovely, manly length of him. His taut stomach. Long legs in jeans. Even his bare feet fascinated her. What a size they were.

And it was absolutely amazing to know that Ed had come all this way to see her. Not to boss her around, but to help her. Again.

She'd run away from him once and lived to regret it, and it was a miracle that he knew this and had still come back to her.

On many levels it didn't make sense, but Ed had told her he would explain. Now, however, he rose from the sofa and stood square in front of Milla. He was touching close, kissing close, and she was naked beneath her towel, and Ed didn't look like a man intent on explanations.

Milla's heart skipped several beats. *Ask him why he's here.*

He smiled at her. 'Am I right in assuming that we're safely past the first date?'

'That's a funny question,' she said, thrown by its unexpectedness. 'Are you angling for another kiss?'

Ed touched her on the elbow, and that simplest contact sent rivers of heat under her towel.

'Must admit, I'm not in the habit of asking.'

She was sinking beneath his spell. *I should be demanding answers. Now. Before it's too late.*

But Ed was already moving in closer and he spoke softly, next to her ear. 'I've missed you, bakery girl.'

I've missed you, too. So, so much.

If she let Ed kiss her now, she knew she would end up in bed with him, and, oh, Lordy, she was melting at the very thought. But she also knew very well that she would end up more deeply in love with this gorgeous man. And how could she let that happen when there were still so many unanswered questions between them?

With huge reluctance, she placed her hands firmly in the centre of his chest, holding him at bay. 'Ed, we haven't talked yet. You haven't told me why you've come back.'

He gave a choked groan.

'It's a fair question,' she said defensively.

His response was a wry, sad smile. 'Milla, give a man a break. You're standing here in nothing but a towel. You're driving me wild, and you want to interrogate me.'

'It's not that I want— It—it's just that—' Her head was swimming. Her hands were still pressed against the brick wall of his chest, holding him away from her, but what she really wanted was to have him close again. Holding her.

She couldn't stop thinking about his farewell kiss. She wanted his arms around her, his lips sealed to hers.

And before she'd properly sorted her thoughts, Ed covered her hands with his own, folding them, holding them against his shirt.

'I have questions, too,' he said softly. 'I need to know if I still terrify you.'

She was sinking fast. 'You don't,' she whispered.

And then…he touched his lips to hers, just the briefest, softest brush… 'What about now?'

Already, she was halfway to meltdown. 'No. Not scared.'

'And now?' he asked, drawing her into his arms.

Now, she was lost in a blaze of longing. She wanted his lips, his hands, his body.

'Not afraid,' she whispered in a breathy gasp as she slipped her arms around his neck, as she looked clear into his eyes and lifted her lips to meet his.

The first mouth-to-mouth touch was magic. It ignited the fire she'd felt on the night of their very first kiss all those years ago, inducing a jolting reaction that rendered her reckless and wanton.

She felt no fear. This was the man who'd worked side by side with her today. The man who'd travelled hemispheres to be with her for this first important day. When he picked her up and carried her to the bedroom, she couldn't find a single reason to resist. She simply gave a soft yearning sigh and pressed her lips against his neck.

Ed lowered her to the bed and he looked down at her, and his eyes were shiny as he traced his fingertips over her heated skin, following the edge of the knotted towel.

'You're so beautiful,' he said softly. 'I'll never forget the first time I saw you in London. I wanted to make you mine straight away.'

She knew she would cry if she thought about the wrong paths she'd taken, so she pulled him down to her and kissed him again, kissed him long and hard till the aching knot of tears in her throat eased.

Oh, how she loved the taste and feel of him. On a wave of rekindled need, she slipped her hands under his T-shirt and slid her palms over his smooth, warm skin, over his muscly shoulders that she'd admired so often.

Impatient now, she helped Ed out of his T-shirt and her heat and longing mounted as he lowered his jeans.

His eyes were smouldering now as he flipped the ties on her towel, and Milla took a deep breath as it fell away. For a scant moment she felt vulnerable beneath his smoky gaze, but as he let his palm glide over the curve of her hip he let out a soft, deeply appreciative sigh. And this time, when he leaned in to kiss her, she felt both safe and triumphant.

She belonged in Ed's arms. He belonged in her bed. They made love with desperate need and with the excitement of new discovery that was interlaced with heart-lifting moments of exquisite tenderness.

With each murmured endearment, with each kiss and touch, Ed took her to new heights of pleasure and release, and she cried from the sheer, piercing joy of it.

Afterwards, she lay for ages with her head on his chest, listening as the drumming of his heartbeats slowed.

And then she turned to him. 'I guess that's answered your question.'

He fingered a tendril of hair from her forehead. 'So you're still OK?'

She'd never had such an attentive and considerate, sexy lover. 'I'm certainly OK, Ed. I'm very OK.' She didn't think she'd ever felt so OK.

He'd made this long day perfect.

CHAPTER ELEVEN

Twilight had given way to night.

Milla turned on a bedside lamp, rolled out of the bed and stood smiling down at Ed. 'You must be hungry.'

He gave a soft laugh. He hadn't given dinner a thought. He was still floating on a cloud of warm elation, still coming to terms with the surprising turn this day had taken.

So much for his plans to take things slowly with Milla...

No wonder people used terms like bewitched and black magic to explain explosive attraction. From the moment he'd touched her he'd been a lost man.

Now, she shot him an exceptionally happy grin as she pulled on jeans and a white sweater.

'Come downstairs, when you're ready,' she said. 'Hungry or not, I'm making dinner.'

From the doorway, she looked back at him over her shoulder and her green eyes flashed a warning. 'And over dinner, I guess you'd better tell me exactly what you're doing back here in Australia.'

Fair enough, Ed thought. He only hoped he could tell his story in a way that convinced her.

There was a storm outside now and sheets of rain

lashed at the windows in wintry gusts as he came down the stairs. The bakery was warm, though, and filled with glowing light as well as the fragrant aroma of simmering tomatoes and herbs.

'Pasta OK for dinner?' Milla asked as she set a pot of water on the stove.

'You must be tired of cooking.'

She shrugged. 'Not really.' She turned the gas high, set a lid on the pot, gave the sauce in the other pot a stir. 'Would you like a glass of wine?'

'To celebrate your successful first day?'

Her eyes danced. 'I think we deserve to celebrate, don't you?'

'Sure.'

They grinned happily at each other once again, and Milla reached for a bottle of rich dark red wine and poured it into two glasses.

'Thanks for your help, Ed.' She handed a glass to him, and her eyes held a dancing smile. 'Thanks for everything.'

A look passed between them that made Ed's heart leap. 'Congratulations to our master baker!' he said.

They clinked glasses and drank, and their smiles held echoes of the new intimacy they'd so recently shared.

'So, I haven't asked,' Ed said as Milla turned her attention to the cooking pot. 'Are you happy with the day's takings?'

'Very happy. We've sold out of almost everything, and people are already starting to leave orders.'

'That's fabulous.'

'I know.' She gave a little skip of triumph. 'I did it! *We* did it.'

But then her expression sobered. She turned from the

stove and picked up her glass, looked down at it, and seemed to study it for a minute or two. Then she lifted her gaze to look directly at him. 'So,' she said quietly, with a worried little smile. 'Are you going to tell me now exactly why you've come back here?'

He knew it was vital that he got his answer right, and he told her the simplified truth. 'As I said before, I've missed you.'

Her eyes widened. And despite their recent love-making, pink bloomed in her cheeks and she took a deep sip of wine.

'I like being with you, Milla. I've always liked being with you.'

Her small smile flickered and vanished like a snuffed candle, and she quickly looked down at her glass again, carefully running her finger around its rim. 'That's nice, Ed. I—I really like being with you, too. But I'd like to understand more. I mean—I'm assuming this is another quick visit? You're an American high-flyer, after all. So what's happening with your business? How can you afford to be here when you've just escaped a takeover by the skin of your teeth?'

'They're all valid questions. And I want to explain. Honestly, I've always planned to explain. It's a long-ish story, though.'

'I'd like to hear it.'

And so Ed told her.

Milla served up their food in deep dishes and they dragged out stools and sat at the bench, sipping wine and swirling rich pasta with their forks, while he told her about his father and Maddie Brown and how their story had lit all kinds of lightbulbs for him. He told her about his grandparents and the farm in Michigan, about the apple orchards and the red barn, and the long summer afternoons beside the Kalamazoo River.

'I've spent my whole life trying to please my father,' he said. 'I've worked as hard as I could at the business, always hoping for some small sign of approval from him. And then I realised in the middle of the Cleaver takeover that my heart wasn't really in it. If I hadn't been so worried about our employees' futures, I could have let the company go.' Ed snapped his fingers. 'Just like that.'

Milla blinked. 'But you were always so dedicated.'

He let out a heavy sigh. 'It was the shock of my life to find out that Cavanaugh Enterprises was all about my father's ego. Or at least, to discover that he could turn his back on it in a heartbeat.'

'For Maddie Brown?' Milla finished softly.

Ed nodded.

She looked thoughtful as she gathered up their plates and carried them to the dishwasher. 'So what's happening to the company now?'

'Just before I left, I settled new negotiations with Cleaver and we're now prepared to let them take over as long as they can guarantee that they'll retain all our employees.'

Milla's face was pale. 'You've handed your company over?'

'Yes.'

'And then rushed straight here?'

'Yes.'

She was shaking her head now. 'But that's crazy, Ed. You can't be thinking straight. You can't have thought this through.' Now she was pacing, wringing her hands.

'Milla, it's OK. Don't get upset about this.' Ed tried to reach for her, but she pulled away.

'I'm sorry. I'm worried. Of course I'm worried. When you first came here and found out about my bakery plans, you accused me of having a knee-jerk reaction to Harry and the baby and everything. Maybe you were right, but I'm happy with my choice. But now, I think you're doing the same thing. You're overreacting to your father's news.'

'Well, if I am, it feels damn right.'

'But—' Closing her eyes, she pressed her fingers to her temples. 'I don't think I can take all this in right now.'

'It's been a long day, and I'm sorry, Milla. The last thing I wanted was to add to your worries.' Ed scratched at the annoying, two-day-old roughness on his jaw. 'Maybe you need a good night's sleep. If you like, I can book into the pub.'

'Actually, I've already done that for you, Ed. While you were sleeping.'

He tried not to mind that she was obviously keen to evict him, but he felt as if everything was unravelling. He'd come here to help her, to take things slowly and to explain the whole situation, to share his hopes, his plans, and instead he'd rushed in and bedded her.

Great work, Brainless.

He wished he could expand on his explanation now, wished he could appease Milla's justifiable concerns, but he knew that she must be exhausted. Her day had started at three a.m.

His only option now was to hope that he could find new and better ways to convince her that he cared. Truly cared. That he would never hurt her. But he would have to leave that till tomorrow.

'I'll get my things,' he said and he was up the stairs and back again in a flash.

At the front door, Milla looked miserable. 'If you'd stayed here, Ed, the whole town would know about it by morning.'

'Of course. Best to avoid the small-town gossip.' He pulled on his jacket.

She opened the door a chink. It was still windy and rainy outside, and she chewed anxiously at her lip. 'The people in this town have already plied me with questions about the nice American.'

He couldn't bring himself to smile. 'It's OK. You don't have to justify sending me to the pub.' He kissed her cheek. 'Don't worry about any of this. Get a good night's sleep.'

She nodded. 'You, too.'

'See you in the morning.' Ed set off, head down, into the rainy night, with the grim sense that he was dangling over a precipice.

Milla closed the door and leaned back against it, closing her eyes, wishing she didn't feel so unbearably lonely now. In her head she knew she'd done the right thing by sending Ed away. She had to protect herself.

She just wished her heart could agree.

Don't think about him. Just go to sleep...

Heaven knew she desperately needed sleep. She'd had a huge day, the biggest day of her life, and there would be another one just like it tomorrow.

But how could she sleep now? she wondered as she trudged back upstairs. In a few short hours, Ed had swept back into her life and he'd completely stolen her heart. But he'd left her mind whirling with a thousand thoughts and questions.

She'd been a fool to start kissing him and more or less lure him into her bed *before* she'd asked *all* her questions. If only she'd heard his impossible story first.

The idea of Ed Cavanaugh walking away from his family business was incredible. The thought of him leaving New York was impossible.

And now she felt guilty and worried that she'd unwittingly lured him here. Had she somehow given him the wrong signals?

Or were they, miraculously, the right signals?

Her mind was whirling with fatigue and nervous exhaustion as she tried to sort out the bare facts.

Ed was attracted to her, certainly. No doubt about that. And he'd amazed her this morning with his help in the bakery.

But what was one morning? One night?

She was planning to put down roots here. She would be working in the bakery day after day, week after week, and Ed's interest could be nothing more than temporary at best.

And yet, knowing this, Milla had helplessly fallen in love with him. Even now, she felt swoony and breathless whenever she thought about his lovemaking. But how could she have made such a foolish mistake?

Arrgh. She had no chance of going to sleep.

The alarm sounded at three a.m.

Milla dragged herself out of bed and didn't allow herself to think about the hours of sleep she'd missed. She dressed quickly, pulled her hair into a scrunchie, splashed her face with cold water and hurried down-stairs.

Just as she had yesterday, she flicked on the lights and filled the kettle, and like yesterday there was a knock at the door.

Her stomach flipped. She hadn't really expected Ed to turn up so early.

When she opened the door and saw him standing there, tall, dark and hunky, eyes holding a cautious smile, she felt her heart twist as if he'd skewered it.

'Top o' the morning,' he said and his breath made a puff of white cloud in the frosty air.

He smiled at her, smiled with his eyes, as if he was asking her to trust him.

I want to, Ed. So much.

She let him in and closed the door quickly. 'I hope you've caught up on your jet lag,' she said.

'I feel fine,' he answered quickly. 'How about you?'

'I'm fine,' she lied, suspecting that he'd lied, too. There were shadows beneath his eyes that hadn't been there yesterday.

'So, is it the same routine today?' he asked as they made their respective mugs of tea and coffee again, and Milla collected yeast and water.

'That's right.' She felt an urge to touch him, to give him a tiny sign of hope, but she made herself be sensible. 'You can put in two bags of flour whenever you're ready, thanks.'

At least, her spirits lifted once again as the ingredients began to mix. She was determined to enjoy this second day, despite her tiredness, despite her nagging worry that Ed was about to shatter her heart.

She knew she loved him, and she suspected that Ed

believed he loved her, but she couldn't take off and spend her life with him. She was committed to this place now and she really wanted to make it work. The alternative option of Ed Cavanaugh settling down in the Bellaroo Bakery was positively ludicrous.

An overwhelming attraction wasn't enough to bridge the huge gap between their lifestyles and allegiances. Even love wasn't enough. Last night Milla had been round and round this problem, rolling and pummelling it like kneaded dough, but this morning she knew there was no solution.

In a way, she was grateful for the hard work ahead of her today. She had to give one hundred per cent concentration to every task, couldn't afford a single mistake. Each loaf and bun and pie had to be perfect.

One thing she couldn't deny—Ed really stepped up to the plate. As an assistant on his second day, he couldn't be faulted. He was a quick learner, of course, and his aim was to lighten her load. Which he did in a thousand and one small ways.

'I reckon you could easily sell at least another dozen bread loaves,' decided Carol, who'd been working in the shopfront, and had made a list for Milla, which she presented at the end of the day.

'White and grainy are the most popular,' she said. 'And pies. By crikey, those Main Roads guys bought up almost all your pies in one hit.'

'What about the sweet things?' Milla asked.

'Well, we have six advance orders for cherry lattice pies for the weekend already.'

Milla laughed. 'I can see what I'll be doing on Saturday mornings from now on.'

'You're going to need to train an apprentice,' suggested Ed.

She nodded tiredly. 'One step at a time.' She rubbed at the back of her neck, trying to ease a nagging headache.

'You should put your feet up. It's my turn to shout dinner,' he said.

'That'd be nice, but I think I should go for a run again. The fresh air will clear the cobwebs.' *And with luck it will tire me out completely.*

'I'll join you.'

That wasn't what she'd planned and she almost protested. All day she'd been super-aware of Ed. Every glance, each exchange, every time they touched, even an accidental connection like bumping elbows, she'd felt a flash of heat, a clutch of longing.

She'd hoped to gain a little clarity and distance on this run. But after the big day Ed had put in to help her, she couldn't reject his company now, especially when she knew he was used to attending the gym and going for regular runs.

'That'd be great,' she said. 'See you in ten.' And she went upstairs to change into a tracksuit and joggers.

At least the rain had stopped, but it was a cold grey dusk with no sign of a sunset as they set off, running down a dirt road and dodging puddles.

Ed matched his stride to Milla's and they jogged side by side along the empty road, past wheat fields and paddocks of sheep where kangaroos grazed in the shadowy verges. When the road dipped to cross a creek, they found stepping stones, then picked up their pace and ran on.

Apart from the thudding of their footsteps, the only sound was the keening cry of a lone falcon circling high above them, floating on the wind.

It was almost dark when Ed saw the sign on the edge of the road. Milla had been pushing herself to keep up with him and she was quietly relieved when he slowed down.

'Hang on,' he said. 'I'd like to check this out.'

'You planning to buy a farm, Ed?' she joked as she stood beside him, hands on hips, panting slightly.

'Just curious.'

'This is the Johnsons' place.'

'You know it?'

Milla nodded. 'As far as I remember, it was a good farm. A mix of sheep and wheat. Lovely homestead.'

He turned to her with a smile. 'I saw the house up on the rise back there. Lots of trees.' There was a silvery flash of excitement in his grey eyes.

'But you're not looking at property, are you?' Milla was suddenly uncertain again.

Instead of answering her, Ed just stood there, staring at the sign.

'Ed, what's this about? Why are you suddenly interested in a farm?'

'I'd like to take a closer look,' he said. 'You know me, always on the lookout for a good investment.' But he said this with a shrug, as if he was trying to make light of it.

She was definitely uneasy now. 'You're not thinking of buying it?' The possibility made her head spin.

'Don't look so worried.'

But she *was* worried. Worried that Ed was getting

carried away. Worried that he was acting completely out of character and rushing headlong into disaster.

'We should be heading back,' she said. 'It's almost dark.'

'You're right,' he agreed, but with clear reluctance. 'We can talk about the farm when we get back.'

Milla worried the whole way back to town.

She deliberately 'dressed down' for dinner, choosing an unromantic turtle-neck black sweater and jeans. It was time for another round of straight shooting with Ed. She couldn't afford another night of emotional turmoil.

She'd agreed to meet him in the pub's dining room, so she was surprised when she found him waiting on her doorstep. Again.

'Slight change of plans.' He gave her a jagged smile as he held out a metal container. 'Hope you don't mind, but I talked the chef into giving me a takeout dinner. Thought we could use a little privacy.'

Privacy...

Milla was slugged by equal jolts of delight and dismay. Privacy with Ed could be fabulous, but also dangerous. At least she was on guard tonight, and she knew she had to seize this chance to set the record straight with him.

'So what are we eating?' she asked as she led him back inside.

'Salt and pepper calamari and Chinese greens.'

'Yum. Good choice. I've just realised how hungry I am.'

She found plates and cutlery and set them on the bench, while Ed grabbed a serving spoon and ladled out generous helpings. The cat came meowing around their legs.

'There might be leftovers if you're lucky,' Ed told Blue, who settled to purr sleepily at their feet.

Milla tried not to think about how cosy and familiar and downright pleasant this dining arrangement was. And she also tried to ignore how attractive Ed looked, showered and shaved, sitting opposite her in a dark V-necked cashmere sweater over a blue and white striped, collared shirt. She had to ignore the enticing whiffs of his aftershave, too, had to forget how positively blissful he'd been in bed.

It was time to focus on setting him straight.

Perhaps he sensed this. He was more subdued as they started eating, and Milla didn't want to spoil their digestion, so she kept their conversation light and easy while they ate, filling Ed in with news about Heidi and Brad and their children, about her parents, about the Joneses in the general store and how helpful they'd been.

But eventually they finished eating and Ed collected their plates and took them over to the sink. Then he came back and sat on a stool, choosing the one beside Milla rather than opposite.

He was smiling, but the smile was a little grim around the edges, and he zeroed straight in on the topic they'd been avoiding all day.

'We've got to talk about us, haven't we?'

'We have,' Milla said softly as tension tightened knots in her stomach. 'I must admit, I'm still very confused about why you're here.'

'I'm not,' he said quietly. 'I know exactly why I'm here.'

Her heart drummed hard.

'It's simple,' Ed said and the look in his eyes was both tender and fierce. 'I want you.'

Those three words *I want you* speared deep inside her, stirring a longing so deep and painful she almost wept. *I want you, too.*

But how was it possible?

'Any terms,' Ed went on. 'Any conditions. You on your native soil. Wherever you want to be, I want to be there with you, Milla.'

Tears filled her eyes. She felt thrilled and scared at once. Ed was reaching for the impossible, trying to make it sound workable.

'I was planning to court you,' he said. 'You know... the unrushed, old-fashioned, patient style of courting.'

She managed to smile at this. 'Isn't that supposed to happen before you rush a girl into bed?'

'That's the general advice.' Reaching for her hand, he looked down at it as he cradled it in his large palm. 'The thing is, Milla, I'm not just crazy in love with you. You've taught me things.'

She knew she looked surprised. She couldn't imagine what he meant.

'When I was here before,' he said. 'You talked about self-worth and you set me thinking. I've asked myself what I needed to change, if I wanted to be someone I really liked. If I wanted to *do* something that felt right. Felt good. Worthwhile. And every time the answer was the same.'

'And it had nothing to do with being CEO of Cavanaugh Enterprises,' Milla guessed.

'Damn right.'

She was remembering now how Ed's eyes had shone when he'd talked about his grandparents in Michigan.

She remembered finding the shaving brush that he'd almost left behind on his last visit.

I've kept it as a kind of reminder of the old guy. I—I guess I wanted to be like him.

At the time she'd told him: *You might be more like him than you realise.*

'So, is this the real Ed Cavanaugh?' she asked softly.

'I think it must be.' Ed gave a shaky laugh. 'We can make it work. I know it.'

The sincerity in his eyes was unmistakable. It filled her with golden light. With sudden glorious courage. 'I believe you.'

She did. At last, amazingly, she truly did believe.

'The main thing is I love you, Milla. I'm hoping against hope that you might love me. I—I know we Cavanaughs have—'

'Shh.' Milla slipped from her stool and took both his hands in hers. 'Let's not talk about Cavanaugh history tonight.'

Ed had gone out of his way to prove his love for her through word and deed, and now she lifted his hands to her lips and kissed his fingers.

Looking up, she smiled bravely, confidently into his eyes. 'I love you too, Ed. I've been scared to admit it, but I know that's crazy considering that I actually fell for you on the first night we met.'

Feeling light-hearted with happiness and certainty now, she slipped her arms around his neck. 'I—I adore everything about you, you gorgeous man. How you look, how you move, how you think, how you kiss. And now you've gone out of your way to help me, and—'

She didn't quite get to the end of her soliloquy. Ed

cut off her words with the most beautiful of kisses, on her lips, on her chin, her neck…

And they didn't finish that particular conversation for a very long time.

By then, their clothes were scattered on the floor and they were curled close in bed, and, having just made love again, they were exceptionally happy and sleepy.

'You realise we now have a second chance to get this right,' Ed said softly.

'Yes.' Milla nestled, deep and warm into the cay of his shoulder. 'This is how we were meant to be.'

'I couldn't let you go a second time.'

Milla smiled up at him. 'I'm so glad you're persistent.'

After a bit, she said sleepily, 'I'm still worried that you haven't thought the bakery part through, though. I can't believe you'll want to work in a bakery for ever.'

'You're right,' he admitted. 'That's why I've checked out the Johnsons' farm.'

'Already?'

He dropped a kiss on her frowning forehead. 'When I went back to the hotel, I stole a quick look on the Internet. The farm has nine dams and a creek, eleven well-fenced paddocks, a machinery shed, three silos…'

Milla tried, unsuccessfully, to hold onto her frown, but a smile broke through. 'And what would you grow in these eleven well-fenced paddocks?'

'Sheep. Organic wheat. Heirloom varieties.'

'So I could bake it?'

Gently, he brushed a strand of hair from her cheek. 'I thought we could employ an artisan baker.'

'But I've only just started.'

'Well, we're certainly going to need another baker when we start our family.'

She'd been on the brink of a yawn, but now her sleepiness vanished in a flash of excitement. 'You want a family?'

'We have to help fill the Bellaroo Creek school, don't we?' Ed drew her into his arms again. 'Isn't it our mission to rescue this town?'

'I knew there was another reason why I loved you.'

EPILOGUE

MILLA SAT ON the edge of the hospital bed, dressed and ready to leave. She was too excited to bother about morning tea. She just wanted to gaze and gaze at the sweet precious bundle in her arms.

Her baby's name was Katie Margaret, named after Ed's paternal grandmother and Milla's mum. She had dark hair like her daddy's and the cutest, neat little nose and ears and the daintiest mouth and hands and feet.

Perfection, in other words, from head to toe.

And now, the little girl yawned and stretched. *Just like Ed,* Milla thought with a happy grin.

Right on cue, her husband appeared in the doorway. 'How are my bride and my firstborn?' he asked, striding into the room proud as punch.

'Ready and raring to go.' Milla flushed with happiness as he came in and kissed her. Ed was still the best-looking guy she'd ever met.

'Has Katie grown while I've been away?' He leaned down to make cooing noises at his daughter.

'I'm sure she's definitely grown cuter and brighter overnight.'

'Spoken like a very proud mom.'

But now, Ed's grey eyes searched Milla's face, as if

he wanted to make sure she really was OK. He'd been a little shaken by the whole business of birthing and he seemed to find it hard to believe she'd bounced back so quickly.

'How's everything at the bakery?' she asked to divert him.

'Absolutely fine. Cooper's managing brilliantly.'

Cooper Jackson, a former shearer's cook, had taken to baking like the proverbial duck to water. Training him had been Milla's latest project. And she and Ed had also sponsored him to have extra experience at an organic bakery in Tasmania. Now he was living in the rooms above their shop and running the show.

'Hey, sweet pea.' Ed touched Katie's hand, watching her tiny fingers unfurl and stretch. 'Ready to come home?'

'Home to a nursery that your daddy has painted from top to bottom and made fit for a princess?' added Milla.

'Home to baby lambs, and a black and white dog and a ginger cat,' said Ed, who was truly in his element now that he was a farmer, a husband *and* a father.

Milla was bursting with happiness, too. She had to pinch herself as she looked around at the profusion of flowers and cards and stuffed toys that had been sent or hand delivered by family members and friends and customers from the bakery.

She couldn't help remembering that other lonely time, over two years ago now, when she'd sat in a bleak, empty hospital room, grieving for her lost baby, and wondering what on earth she would do with the rest of her sad, sorry life.

'I've brought boxes to cart all these things,' Ed said

as he began to gather up the bouquets. 'I'll take them to the car and come back for you. You'll soon be home.'

Home. Their favourite place to be.

They drove from the hospital in Parkes, with Katie safely in her little capsule in the back of their all-wheel drive. Home through the familiar countryside, with fields of wheat shimmering in the soft breeze and with ewes and new lambs grazing in the morning sunlight.

Home to a sprawling low weatherboard house, painted white and surrounded by wisteria-covered trellises, flower gardens and trees.

They adored their comfy, rambling farmhouse with its sunny, north-facing kitchen and its huge fireplace for winter. Together they'd established the vegetable gardens and chickens that Milla had always wanted, as well as a newly planted orchard that meant so much to Ed.

And now a spare bedroom had been painted white with bright colourful trims.

As Ed turned off the main road down the gravel road to their farm Milla felt a rush of happiness and a sense of fulfilment beyond her wildest dreams.

Her parents were arriving in two days' time to admire their granddaughter and to help her settle into motherhood. Gerry and Maddie Cavanaugh were coming the following month. Since Ed's marriage they'd come down under every six months, alternating with Ed and Milla's trips to the US, and each time Milla and Ed saw Gerry he seemed happier and more deeply content.

'All Maddie's work,' he told them with a grin.

'Now,' said Ed as he pulled up at the front of their house. 'There's one more surprise here for you.'

She grinned, thinking of more long-stemmed roses. Or perhaps a bottle of champagne.

'You won't have to cook for the next three months,' Ed said.

Milla blinked at him. 'Are you offering to look after our meals?'

'I don't have to. Our freezer's full to overflowing. Just about every housewife in the district has turned up here with a foil-covered casserole.'

'Wow,' Milla said softly. 'That's amazing.'

'Not so amazing considering everything you've done for this community.'

Perhaps that was true, but it had all been fun.

Milla suspected that she would remember this moment for ever as she climbed out of the vehicle and as she watched Ed carefully extract their baby girl from her capsule. Her heart was as light as a dawn breeze as she hooked her arm through her husband's and the three of them went inside.

* * * * *

Mills & Boon® Hardback
August 2013

ROMANCE

The Billionaire's Trophy	Lynne Graham
Prince of Secrets	Lucy Monroe
A Royal Without Rules	Caitlin Crews
A Deal with Di Capua	Cathy Williams
Imprisoned by a Vow	Annie West
Duty At What Cost?	Michelle Conder
The Rings that Bind	Michelle Smart
An Inheritance of Shame	Kate Hewitt
Faking It to Making It	Ally Blake
Girl Least Likely to Marry	Amy Andrews
The Cowboy She Couldn't Forget	Patricia Thayer
A Marriage Made in Italy	Rebecca Winters
Miracle in Bellaroo Creek	Barbara Hannay
The Courage To Say Yes	Barbara Wallace
All Bets Are On	Charlotte Phillips
Last-Minute Bridesmaid	Nina Harrington
Daring to Date Dr Celebrity	Emily Forbes
Resisting the New Doc In Town	Lucy Clark

MEDICAL

Miracle on Kaimotu Island	Marion Lennox
Always the Hero	Alison Roberts
The Maverick Doctor and Miss Prim	Scarlet Wilson
About That Night...	Scarlet Wilson

0713 GEN STD HB

Mills & Boon® Large Print
August 2013

ROMANCE

Master of her Virtue	Miranda Lee
The Cost of her Innocence	Jacqueline Baird
A Taste of the Forbidden	Carole Mortimer
Count Valieri's Prisoner	Sara Craven
The Merciless Travis Wilde	Sandra Marton
A Game with One Winner	Lynn Raye Harris
Heir to a Desert Legacy	Maisey Yates
Sparks Fly with the Billionaire	Marion Lennox
A Daddy for Her Sons	Raye Morgan
Along Came Twins…	Rebecca Winters
An Accidental Family	Ami Weaver

HISTORICAL

The Dissolute Duke	Sophia James
His Unusual Governess	Anne Herries
An Ideal Husband?	Michelle Styles
At the Highlander's Mercy	Terri Brisbin
The Rake to Redeem Her	Julia Justiss

MEDICAL

The Brooding Doc's Redemption	Kate Hardy
An Inescapable Temptation	Scarlet Wilson
Revealing The Real Dr Robinson	Dianne Drake
The Rebel and Miss Jones	Annie Claydon
The Son that Changed his Life	Jennifer Taylor
Swallowbrook's Wedding of the Year	Abigail Gordon

Mills & Boon® Hardback
September 2013

ROMANCE

Challenging Dante	Lynne Graham
Captivated by Her Innocence	Kim Lawrence
Lost to the Desert Warrior	Sarah Morgan
His Unexpected Legacy	Chantelle Shaw
Never Say No to a Caffarelli	Melanie Milburne
His Ring Is Not Enough	Maisey Yates
A Reputation to Uphold	Victoria Parker
A Whisper of Disgrace	Sharon Kendrick
If You Can't Stand the Heat...	Joss Wood
Maid of Dishonour	Heidi Rice
Bound by a Baby	Kate Hardy
In the Line of Duty	Ami Weaver
Patchwork Family in the Outback	Soraya Lane
Stranded with the Tycoon	Sophie Pembroke
The Rebound Guy	Fiona Harper
Greek for Beginners	Jackie Braun
A Child to Heal Their Hearts	Dianne Drake
Sheltered by Her Top-Notch Boss	Joanna Neil

MEDICAL

The Wife He Never Forgot	Anne Fraser
The Lone Wolf's Craving	Tina Beckett
Re-awakening His Shy Nurse	Annie Claydon
Safe in His Hands	Amy Ruttan

0813 GEN STD HB

ROMANCE

A Rich Man's Whim	Lynne Graham
A Price Worth Paying?	Trish Morey
A Touch of Notoriety	Carole Mortimer
The Secret Casella Baby	Cathy Williams
Maid for Montero	Kim Lawrence
Captive in his Castle	Chantelle Shaw
Heir to a Dark Inheritance	Maisey Yates
Anything but Vanilla...	Liz Fielding
A Father for Her Triplets	Susan Meier
Second Chance with the Rebel	Cara Colter
First Comes Baby...	Michelle Douglas

HISTORICAL

The Greatest of Sins	Christine Merrill
Tarnished Amongst the Ton	Louise Allen
The Beauty Within	Marguerite Kaye
The Devil Claims a Wife	Helen Dickson
The Scarred Earl	Elizabeth Beacon

MEDICAL

NYC Angels: Redeeming The Playboy	Carol Marinelli
NYC Angels: Heiress's Baby Scandal	Janice Lynn
St Piran's: The Wedding!	Alison Roberts
Sydney Harbour Hospital: Evie's Bombshell	Amy Andrews
The Prince Who Charmed Her	Fiona McArthur
His Hidden American Beauty	Connie Cox